SUN BLEACHED SCARECROWS

James Jenkins

Front cover image by the publisher.

Book design by the publisher.

ISBN: 9798375640235

AP

FOR JOEY AND RENDY

Phylloscopus Collybita Tristis

Detective Constable Austin Healey peered through the binoculars

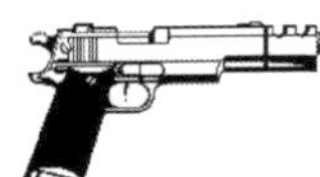

as his heart bounced excitably. The practiced breathing intended for this such scenario was being put to the test as the adrenaline flowed around his body, it was all he could do to stay motionless. He blended in with the wet earth and fallen bracken. The expensive, all-in-one Ghillie suit wouldn't have looked out of place in a B-Movie horror film – it disguised him perfectly. Ever since getting the tip off on the target, Austin Healey had planned for this night. Finally, he could cross this one off the list. He watched the treeline under the canopy of leaves careful not to make any sound adjusting the binoculars. It didn't matter if he was missing the works party for this. Too long he'd waited for this moment and besides, it wasn't like any of his colleagues would miss him. Austin wasn't what you would call popular.

He had joined the police force with high hopes, it would be the start to a new life where he could be respected for wanting to uphold justice. He'd looked forward to making a real difference with likeminded colleagues but all he found along the way was corruption, bullying and favouritism. The latter he'd never possessed, the bullying was plenty. It reminded him more of past school days and his time as a prefect. Austin had never been able to comprehend why his strict code of honesty and the upholding of his moral obligation to law isolated him from fellow officers. Yes, there had been many times where his information led to disciplinaries – suspensions – and one dishonourable discharge. But that was justice. Yet this only served to distance him further from the affections of his superiors and even worse, overlooked for promotion. How he wished the Internal Investigation Division would recognise his good work. The filthy law breaking he'd witnessed from his own colleagues. Men and women who were bound by a sacred honour, brazenly flaunting the law. He'd seen it all, from accepting free breakfasts to allowing offenders to go with no charge! Austin only recently watched an officer of the law letting a female driver go after being stopped for using a mobile phone. In the process she almost mounted the curb and hit an old lady. Almost but not. Still, laws were meant to be followed as far as Austin was concerned. His partner had taken the lead. Austin watched from the police car, unable to believe the vile abuse of law. The fellow officer was brazenly laughing with the offender, leaning against her car in a relaxed manner. He took something from the woman as she passed it out of the window. The officer tapped the roof of her car and waved – his smile spread from ear to ear like the Cheshire cat. Austin's partner produced a piece of folded up paper. "Got her number! She was well fit mate, I'm gonna smash the fuck out of that." Naturally it was only Detective Constable Austin Healy's obligation to take this information to his boss, Chief Superintendent Carl Bragg. His superior wasn't impressed. Austin handed in an official complaint. It would mean Bragg would have to deal with the officer – who he was quite fond of – and discipline him to the letter of the law. To Austin's chagrin, he was rewarded with a reassignment to a desk for two months. Maybe he was just in the wrong department he wondered? Surely this sort of treatment wasn't usual across the entire British Police Force? Tonight, he cast frustrations aside, for he was close to his target.

The tree branch shook slightly in front of him, it wasn't a gust of wind. The air had been still all night, almost unusually. No, this was it. Adjusting the binoculars, he took a deep breath to steady his vision not wanting to miss his chance. Suddenly he was startled to the sound of something crashing through the undergrowth.

"Come on! Do me here you dirty bastard. This is what you paid me for innit?" the plump and scantily dressed woman said as she trailed off with a filthy laugh. An older man pounding his hands up and down on his small erect penis, mock chased after her.

"Oh, you dirty minx! Let me spank you with my wicked wand."

Somewhere in between "Dirty" and "Bastard", Austin had seen all his hard work just take off – literally. The unannounced intruders had scared off the rare bird before he could properly focus his camera. Gone! The elusive Phylloscopus Collybita Tristis, or more commonly known as the Siberian Chiffchaff. Well, at least it was in the birdwatching community. This was the very bird Austin had spent hours if not weeks of planning and patience upon and now the two doggers in a sexual fury had ruined everything! The filthy perverts. He would bring them in that was for sure. The woman's claim to have been paid hadn't gone over Austin's head either. He rose from the undergrowth as the couple stopped in stunned horror. The effect was lost on Austin as he hadn't remembered the camouflaged suit he was wearing, to the immobile pair it looked like swamp thing rising from the forest floor. The woman screamed as he read them their rights. "It's a fucking monster!!!"

"Police!" shouted Austin.

The man was not impressed, "Now you look here young man." A sorry looking, erect cock still protruding from his fly. "I don't know your rank or… well who the fuck you are but I'd be careful if I were you, sunshine. Chief Superintendent Carl Bragg happens to be a good friend of mine. Perhaps it would be better if we all just walked away?"

How dare this perv bring his superior into this. Austin was fuming, he didn't care what relationship the depraved sex offender thought he had with Bragg. Austin would make sure this was dealt with using the full force of the law. He finished the arrest and ordered the pair back to the forest visitor's car park. He would have to squeeze them both into the small

Toyota Yaris he owned. It wouldn't win him any fans bringing in an arrest tonight. The staff would be thin on the ground as it was due to the party. Most of his colleagues would have been only too happy to let the perps walk free in exchange for some more drinking time, perhaps some inter-work-related flirting. That was what Austin despised most about the works do.

"What is it you want? Money?" the man asked Austin as he pulled the front seat forward trying to squeeze the large woman into the back. "What the hell were you doing waiting in the woods dressed as a fucking tree anyway?"

"Get in the vehicle sir. You are under arrest, please keep quiet until we get to the station."

"Jobsworth prick," the man muttered. Suddenly Austin felt better about the bird. At least it hadn't all been for nothing. Two arrests for indecent exposure and a possible solicitating offence. A good night's work, or so he thought.

XXX

Less than a week later Austin had again been failed by the hierarchy. Instead of thanks and praise for his off-duty arrest, Austin's superior had been furious.

"Henry Moore! You couldn't pick anyone worse to piss off could you Healey? You total prick. You know who he is don't you?" Chief Superintendent Bragg fumed. Austin did know who Henry Moore was. It had been the first thing he'd found out after taking him in to be charged. The man made a big show about his influence in the police and how he would have Austin's balls fed to various animals. The threats grew in intensity the closer they'd got to the station. Moore was a very influential figure in the local county, his favour was very beneficial to many high-ranking police officers it would seem. His wealth and political attributes had appeared to make him untouchable. Henry Moore had eventually been released after spending four hours in a police cell with a crack head until his lawyer was tracked down. He in turn contacted Chief Superintendent Bragg, who himself had been at the party.

"I'm well aware of who he is sir, no one is excused from violating the law."

"Listen to you Healey. It's that sort of shit talk that isolates you from everyone else. Why does it matter to you so much? Sometimes you've got to let it go. What the bleeding hell were you doing there in the first place? Moore and his bint said you came out of the ground like some fucking human Christmas tree! What the fucking hell were you playing at? You were off duty."

Austin considered his response – he knew that there would be ridicule over his hobby. "I was birdwatching sir."

"You what? You're not one of them bloody twitchers are you? Jesus Christ Healey, I should have seen it before. So, you chose to spend your night hiding in the woods waiting for a bird when you could have been at the party with your colleagues? I'll never understand you Healey…" Bragg paused to shake his head, "Look, I'm going to have to make a bit of a display to Henry Moore. It's only a temporary thing and to be honest with you Constable…"

"Detective Constable, Sir," Austin hastily reminded his boss.

"Yes Healey. Detective constable, it's getting hard to find anyone who will work with you. Some alone time will do you good, I think. I'm going to have you look over some cold cases. Nothing too spectacular and you probably won't find anything, but it keeps you out of the way for a while. Moore will forget about it soon."

That is why he now found himself sifting through low priority cases that lacked any leads. The unsolved crimes passed to him in the file had been minor offences. Skimming through the first three hadn't turned up much more than minor burglaries which were almost always unsolvable. There were two however that intrigued him. A child had been given cocaine at a roadside café, one of the witnesses had given a car registration and description of the suspect's vehicle. Another case he'd skimmed through was reported by a motorist who alleged that they were hit by another car. The offender had driven off before the victim could take the full licence plate. Austin would have discarded the case if It wasn't for the striking similarity in the car's description in both incidents. As well as the partial registration matching the full one, both reports had been made on the same day and within a short distance of each other. It was too much of a coincidence, so why hadn't anyone else run the plates? It was the first thing Austin did and much to his surprise the database showed the registered owner at the time as one Sergeant Paul Hargreaves. Austin had found his case.

The Father

Padre Alvaro opened his bible, he was careful to keep aligned the

additional material inside. He didn't expect any of his disciples to disturb him, but it wouldn't do to be surprised. Years of practiced carefulness wouldn't be for nothing. It wasn't that he preferred the smut magazine to the Lord's words of the bible, but privacy wasn't a virtue at his church. Sure, some of the older ones had become openly curious as to their Padre's visitors over these latter years. The prostitutes he occasionally treated himself to had mostly followed the strict instructions to dress as nuns. This way he could fool the children into thinking they were just missionaries visiting to share the Lord's prayer, there had been one who'd misconstrued his instructions. Instead of turning up dressed as a traditional sister, she'd instead opted to wear a highly inappropriate fetish style nuns' outfit, complete with high heels and suspenders. Luckily, he'd acted quick, ushering the sex worker into his private quarters so that the younger children hadn't time to notice. Alvaro watched the puzzled expressions on a few of the older children. Two in particular, Diego and Estela. The oldest of the orphans living in the long-ago retired monastery. It would have been naïve to think he could keep the pretence up forever, neither of them could be considered children in the eyes of the law anymore. He had toiled over the idea of telling them the truth for some time, but he wanted to protect their innocence for as long as possible. He put them far from his thoughts as he expelled the contents of his epididymis over the big bosomed lady in the glossy magazine. The Padre made a small prayer before wiping himself clean. Letting the familiar feeling of shame wash over him, he lit a cigarette. It wasn't easy being a single parent to twenty-seven children and young adults. In the early days he'd considered playing the dating game, but there never seemed to be any time with children turning up on a regular basis over the years. Alvaro Martinez hadn't asked for any of it. Some fifteen years before, Alvaro had bought the old monastery for a steal. The isolation it provided him with was the perfect place to escape his old life. So far it had worked wonders as a place to hide from the dark life he'd escaped in organised crime. Turning his back on the old ways had been easy, Alvaro himself orphaned before his fifth birthday. He'd endured a tough life on the streets growing up as a beggar and a thief. Later years had seen him become enrolled in street gangs before making his way up the violent chain of command. He'd been clever about his money, putting a bit aside every week until he could finally be free from the city and a life of crime. At first Alvaro had travelled, searching for somewhere he could finally call his own. This had eventually led him to Setinel. A beautiful and isolated town where the locals were simple people who asked few questions. When he bought the crumbling monastery from the local mayor who sold it for a mere pittance (due to Alvaro claiming he was a holy man intending to restore the monastery to its former glory), he never expected to find it already inhabited. The two young children he had found squatting there had reminded Alvaro of himself at that age. The pity within led him to take kindly upon the two youngsters and allowed them to stay as long as they helped with the renovations to the large building. One of the two had been Diego who Alvaro had grown to love like a son. He'd claimed to be a priest to save conflicting stories with the villagers and it had until now at least worked. The small lie had paid off too – quite literally – Locals turned up for a weekly Sunday service and made generous donations for relatively poor folk. It hadn't been all that hard for Alvaro to run the service, in all fairness he actually quite enjoyed the four-hour sessions. As the years passed by, he taught himself more of the bible and respected the code of conduct it promoted. The basic principles had served him well in his teaching to the children, the positive impact on them had been obvious, as it was to Alvaro himself. The special relationship that had developed between Diego and Estela conflicted him however, they were both adults now free to make their own decisions. But on the other hand, Alvaro hadn't ever given the orphans any of the "bees-knees". This part of life he just put on a 'to-do' pile in the furthest reaches of his mind. There could be some comfort taken that the two of them were very responsible and good kids. He'd still make sure to have the chat with them. Just for good measure. It wouldn't be good to ruin what they'd built here. A haven for the unwanted misfits rejected by the rest of society.

After Alvaro found his first residents, they'd numbered only three. But somehow, children kept on turning up, He suspected that the villagers or possibly the two children he'd originally found were passing the children his way. It didn't matter: the loneliness would have sent him mad and the kids gave him purpose. Alvaro wished that there had been a place like the monastery for him when he had been a frightened and deserted child on the streets. There were men who would offer you a place to stay but that came at a violent and degrading price. For Alvaro his intentions were nothing but pure. They were his family and they all behaved like one, he would die for each and every one of them. Most of the orphans had fended for themselves from a very young age. Now, with a little guidance, shelter and food from their crops – they took very little effort to look after. The older ones were always playing the role of big brother or sister, it eased the burden on the former career criminal. The numbers had slowed over the years, less children had come this way which he supposed could be taken as a good sign. The youngest of all the children now was twelve years old and had been the last to arrive, along with his older sister Estela some five years earlier.

A Mother's Love...

Estela hadn't enjoyed a close relationship with her mother. From a young age she'd been used to the successful businesswoman working away in the city. It left her father to take up role of guardian, a loving man who'd given up a successful job in engineering to look after his daughter full time. Not knowing any different, a young Estela led a relatively happy life. Not seeing her mother was normal as was the woman's cold indifference. Her father assured his daughter that her mother was just tired and that it wouldn't be like this forever. But still Estela yearned for a closer bond and tried hard, but no matter how many pictures she drew, her mother regarded her with the same hardness. By the time she reached her seventh birthday, it was evident that the relationship Estela shared with her mother vastly contrasted that of her peers. Now she craved a feminine touch that couldn't always be facilitated by her father. Much to Estela's delight, Mother took a short break from work and the little family travelled to Portugal on holiday. It had been the time of her life, although her mother was still distant, it was at least the most amount of time they had spent together. Even her father seemed the happiest she had ever seen him – until the argument. Thanks to her mother's well-paid job, the large house they stayed in had many rooms. You could almost drown out the shouting if you shut all the doors and put your head under the bed pillows – Estela tried it. It wasn't clear what her parents were arguing about, but it seemed to be about a boy – or boys. She remembered the ones that day – they'd been about her own age. Her mother looked happy watching them play. All three of them had ventured out to the beach for the day. Her mother had been in an unusually good mood, even going so far as to kiss her daughter on the forehead after breakfast – a rare pleasure indeed. The family had walked down to the beach in high spirits. Her parents each took one of her hands and swung her as they walked – Estela had felt true happiness. Her mother had searched for a good spot for them, it was close enough to the shore to swim under adult supervision but closer still to the children's play park. Estela thought it was a great spot. She rushed off into the sea looking back over her shoulder disappointed to see only her father waving. After a short swim, Estela headed back up the beach towards her parents but noticed them both looking very angry with each other. Estela wondered if she should hang back but, in her naivety, thought that perhaps she could help. She stopped a few feet away and listened. Her father was the angriest, he kept saying something about it being weird – something that her mother had done. Also, it had something to do with the boys playing in the nearby play area. Her father seemed upset that his wife had brought them to this spot. Estela liked it. Then her father looked up, noticing her and smiled, ushering her over. He kept saying to her mother "See! See what you have! This is your child." He then began to cry, pulling his daughter close and wrapping her in his loving arms. Her mother had walked back to the holiday home.

That night when the arguing had started again after dinner, Estela had been scared. She didn't understand the adult words and had never seen either of her parents this way so ran to the furthest bedroom. The last words she heard was her mother howling at her father "Why couldn't you give me a boy!" and her father, "Why should it matter?" Estela cried herself to sleep buried under the goose and down feathers.

After the holiday, her mother had gone away. Estela's father had been reassuring about the argument, brushing aside her questions and growing self-doubt. Her mother began to come more at weekends and again Estela embraced the dregs of her attention – although her parents spent most of the time in the bedroom. It was at the beginning of one of these visits that they sat Estela down and told her she was going to have a baby brother. Estela was overjoyed as was her mother who was dancing, hugging and kissing Estela more than ever before. They had felt like a family after that. Her mother came home more often now and talked to Estela more freely, relaxing the formality that she had always regarded her daughter. Estela's father had gone back to work for a while as her mother neared the end of pregnancy, leaving them together for the first time she could remember. Her mother would ask her to carry out meaningless tasks and then tell her strange things that she didn't understand and then – laugh – wickedly. This new way of life went on, her baby brother was born and after a slight respite, her father went back to work. Estela doted over her baby brother and didn't even mind the nappy changes, feeds – and being an emotional punch bag to her mother – she had a family now. Her father worked late and more days of the week – her mother had insisted they needed the money, although her dad kept asking where her mother's money had gone. All Estela knew, he was too tired to play with her now. If he wasn't working or changing Mateo, then he was asleep. She worried for him as he aged before her eyes, no longer the happy energetic man he'd once been.

On Estela's tenth birthday her mother had made a big point of baking Estela a cake. Everyone was getting into the spirit – her father was blowing up balloons and Mateo was knocking them up into the air. Estela was hanging a banner when her mother ushered her over to the kitchen. Eager to accept the bread crumb of attention, Estela obeyed willingly. "Taste this," her mother held out the spoon from the cake mixture and Estela nibbled at it with suspicion. "It's good!" Mother laughed and put some into her own mouth before whispering, "Your dad has some big news. It's a surprise."

They all sat down except her mother who lit the candles and walked over carefully to the table. Everybody was singing as mother set the delicious cake down in front of her – Make a wish! Estela wished to make her mother happy and blew out the candles. "Your father has something he needs to tell you…"

"Maria! Not today! It's her birthday for Christ's sake." Estela saw the anger in her father, he hadn't looked that way since the holiday some years before.

"Tell us Daddy! Tell us!" screamed Mateo excitedly.

Estela herself was now very intrigued and joined in with the chorus "Tell us! Tell us!" Such big news on her birthday could only be good – surely?

Instead, her father got up from the table and stormed off. Estela's mother seized the moment, "Your father is very ill children, he needs an operation but it's very risky… Mateo darling are you okay? Do you want to come hug mummy?" The little lad ran into his mother's arms crying but not truly understanding – Estela did, and nobody offered her a hug.

Eventually her father returned. Mother left them both to talk and took Mateo to bed – she stayed in his room for quite some time. Once Estela was exhausted from interrogating her father, he cradled her whilst she wept. He'd assured her that the operation was the only way and it had a better success rate than Mother had let on. Father had also made her mother apologise for the timing of the news – she abided – reluctantly.

Father's operation came around quickly. Estela had been dreading the day, understanding that it could be the last time she saw him. They had talked at length about the possible outcomes, Father told her to be strong for Mateo and that they must always look after each other. There were no known relatives on her fathers' side, but he mentioned the village he grew up in – Setinel. Estela had agreed to scatter her father's ashes, reluctantly accepting the worst-case scenario. The doctors and nurses had taken him away and just as was feared, she never saw him again. He died on the operating table, which had always been a highlighted scenario. It did little to ease her pain – nor did her mother.

It didn't take long for her mother to rid the house of all things related to her father. Estela had tried to protest but the woman became wicked towards, not physically but using her father's illness against Estela. The woman had shown no sign of grief after her husband's death. If anything, she'd found herself a new freedom often leaving Estela to look after her little brother. Mateo adored his sister and Estela returned that love in full. She knew the little boy was her mother's favourite, so showered with gifts was the boy compared to herself. None of that would have mattered to her, all Estela craved was warmth from her mother and love. The woman had taken care of her since her father's death, but it was strictly essential parenting only – except for her brother. Mateo had been staying in his mother's bed much more frequently, apparently her mother had no limits to the affection she could show the boy.

As Estela's fourteenth birthday approached, her mother had started to see another man. Estela had disliked him straight away – nobody could take her father's place – she sensed there was more to it than that. The feeling appeared to be mutual, so Estela was given her space. Mateo again was showered in gifts but not just from his mother, but the new man too. She never felt jealous. These materialistic presents would have meant nothing. Even when he was allowed to stay in her mother and new lover's bed – still she didn't resent him. He was all she had left of her father. The boy had become more distant as the months went by and Estela found it harder to find time that they could spend together, such was her mother's interference. She had seemed determined to keep them apart. Life dragged on this way, the isolation that Estela suffered made worse by this contrived separation.

One night, her mother hosted a dinner party. Mateo had been allowed downstairs for a while – Estela didn't have to be told she wasn't welcome. Sitting in her room finishing homework, there was a knock at the door. Mateo asked her to come downstairs. Mother wanted her to meet someone. She had followed excitedly, almost unable to believe that her presence was wanted. Her mother and the man sat around the large dining table with other guests. They all stared as Estela walked into the room, her brother scuttling off to mother's side. The woman smirked at her daughter and patted the shoulder of a fat sweaty man sitting to her side, "There Hugo. Isn't she beautiful?"

The man rubbed his hands together and licked his purple rimmed lips before blowing a kiss at Estela. Hugo struggled out of his seat and waddled over to her extending his hand. Courteously, she returned the gesture, his chubby, sweaty hand crushing her own. The way he looked at her should have sent alarm bells ringing, but her mother kept smiling. The man licked his lips again and looked Estela up and down one last time. He wobbled back to the table, "Yes Maria. She's very beautiful indeed."

"Estela, you can go now. Take Mateo, it's his bedtime." Her mother showered her son in kisses. The guests reached out their hands to caress the boy as he walked past them towards his sister.

Estela had put him to bed that night for the first time in a long time. The boy was so much quieter now, he seemed content, but all childish rebellion was missing. He hadn't even argued when Estela turned off his light and returned to her own bedroom.

Her stream of consciousness was broken by the presence of somebody in her room – a man – Father?

A zipper. Heavy breathing. Her eyes adjusted to the darkness. She made out the shape of the fat man shaking something in his hands, but the bedcovers blocked her view. Estela couldn't move. Terror. Hugo began to breath deeper, muttering under his breath between grunts. She closed her eyes tight, as the floorboards began to creak under the weight of the juddering. Suddenly her bedroom door swung open, the fat man a gasp in shock and disappointment. Her mother's voice now, "Hugo! No! Naughty boy. We agreed." Estela kept her eyelids shut but could hear the man pulling up his zipper. "Maria, just a look." Her mother, "You're lucky the girl didn't wake up. Now, come – I think it's time for you to go home."

They left the petrified Estela. She sobbed herself back to sleep. The next morning, she was left to look after Mateo. Nothing was mentioned about the night before, but her mother and new man were in good spirits announcing that they were going to sell the house. That day they would be looking at potential locations. The very idea they would be leaving their family home! But she didn't want to argue today. Getting the woman and her man out of the house was a priority. Estela knew she was in danger, she had promised her father she would protect Mateo. Once they were left alone, she took the opportunity to talk to her brother and find out who the fat man was. Mateo was predictably distant and quiet, to start with, but when Estela had started to cry to him the boy seemed to change. He took on a different role than she'd seen before – a calmness. Estela decided to tell her brother about the strange visit to her bedroom. Reacting as if he was the more experienced older sibling, Mateo then rubbed her shoulders.

"At least they were easy on you for the first time."

Estela's innocence from the previous evening evaporated now knowing what she had shut out of her mind. That's when she knew they had to leave. Not tomorrow or next week but now. Mateo hadn't taken much persuading, once they got talking it became apparent what the poor boy was subjected to. Estela scavenged the house for any money or valuables. She didn't find much but what she had should get them to her father's old village – maybe she would find family there.

XXX

Five years had passed since Mateo and his sister found Alvaro. In that time, Estela had blossomed into a beautiful and caring young lady. Unfortunately, it was her unasked-for beauty, that brought the unwanted attention from the Loco man.

The English man had moved into the villa a few years before. It wasn't uncommon for Alvaro to see people come and go to the usually empty villa. Just a holiday home with the occasional family turning up. This hombre hadn't left after the typical tourist season finished though. The self-proclaimed-Padre hadn't worried. The man had mostly kept to himself, up until now. There were some stories around town, some of the locals had heated incidents with him, most seemed due to the language barrier. A few even claimed the man was responsible for the disappearance of two villagers a year after he arrived. Such rumours were obviously not founded enough for anything other than hearsay. Alvaro would be lying if it hadn't crossed his mind when the Loco man came to visit – so strange was the encounter. He'd been reading in the garden with some of the younger children when the suited individual waltzed in on an authoritative swagger. He made no attempt to speak Spanish and Alvaro's English was limited at best, but he didn't have to be fluent to know he didn't like what he heard. To his understanding the man had been offering Alvaro money for the girl! The level of hate for those who abused him in his youth threatened to boil to the surface. He had to control himself. Estela told him a few days before about how the strange man had followed her home. The first time they had demised that the neighbour was confused about the 'fruit that had been picked' near his land. Even then Alvaro had only fooled himself, he knew what the man really wanted. The stalking had become much more frequent since then. Diego was now becoming restless, the unwanted attention, his would-be girlfriend, Alvaro had warned the boy to leave it alone. He knew too well what love could do to a man, let alone a boy on the cusp of manhood.

It was time he came clean about his past; Diego deserved the truth. The man would be dealt with if he came back, Alvaro hoped it wouldn't come to that, but he would protect his family indefinitely. He knew the look in those eyes, they bore the same darkness he'd seen in many evil souls from his past. The man was clearly dangerous, they would have to know how to protect themselves. So, it was decided, as soon as the boy came back tonight, they would sit down. Alvaro checked the clock on his wall. Diego was late again – young love. He put on his robe and left the sanctuary of the room to check on the other children. As he walked down the corridor, he heard the front door crashing open to the shrieking Estela.

"Padre! Padre! He has Diego!"

Idle Hands

Bobby Cavendish closed his eyes on the sweltering afternoon sun.

His fingers scratched lazily at leathery tanned skin, ushering the flying insect away. Relaxing on the poolside sunbed at the secluded Spanish villa, he took stock of his current dilemma. Since the involuntary yet admittedly essential relocation to the Costa del Sol, life was dull. Oh, he had tried to keep himself busy of course, but the peaceful life now offered was for a man much older than himself. He'd been used to keeping busy with work, it was all he'd known from a young age and in his line of business it had been a twenty-four-seven task. The instructions were to keep a low profile, retire, make the most of the quiet life and in all fairness, this had been a gift not usually extended to men of his nature. But to a man only now knocking on the door of fifty, he felt that there was so much more that he could be doing. The Mediterranean heat coupled with the long hours of isolation had taken its toll on Bobby's sanity too, although he hadn't realised this himself and with nobody around to inform him of the creeping signs of madness, how would he? The locals hadn't been of much help either. Simple folk with a limited grasp on the English language had proven infuriatingly numb of any stimulation. Initially he was far too consumed with grief for the girl he'd never been allowed to declare his undying love. Moving here had seemed the best idea at the time, some good R&R, clarity even. Not being able to enact his revenge was hard to accept. Had it not been for him then that bastard wouldn't have been found! The despair! He didn't even get to end the man's life with his own hands! And how was he rewarded for his troubles? A fucking name. A shit one at that, not that he was able to use it. It hurt Bobby to trade his name with the now deceased policeman. As far as anyone knew, Paul Hargreaves entered Spain through Malaga airport and after that - gone. That was the deal. There was to be no paper trail, no using passports or credit cards. Money was available to him of course but that was done via a fake bank account and those funds had slowly diminished over the last not quite five years. Phipps had visited not long after Bobby moved and that boosted the coffers somewhat. Sometimes it even felt as though he was a prisoner after trading freedom for immunity. He had (in his own eyes) led a relatively quiet life. After arriving at the villa of which had been procured compliments of Paul Hargreaves' nest egg and Chilcot's contacts, all Bobby could do was cry, snort copious amounts of cocaine (yes it really had been that easy to smuggle it on a European flight, it really was) and watch endless romcoms. Once the tears dried up to the sporadic outpour, he'd decided to meet the locals. The town, Setinel, barely a village truth be told, contained a small population. Barely more than sixty excluding the nearby monastery which housed around thirty late teens and young adults as well as the priest. In the early years after the grieving had subsided, Bobby toyed with the idea of taking an interest in asserting some authority on the town. Maybe building a new empire from the ground up, but alas, it wasn't to be. The locals had proven to be peasants, delinquents even. There he had been with plans to accelerate their wealth (and his of course), but none of them possessed a grasp of the English language. They didn't even have the basic teachings of good manners or most importantly, respect. Most of the time he let it go – it was their country – less than a handful of times it proved too much for him. Those unfortunate enough not to entertain his efforts paid the price. It had provided him some ample enjoyment after the grieving. Sensing the growing suspicion from the other villagers persuaded him to move further afield, scouting out the tourism populated seaside towns for his leisure. This still hadn't filled the void – torture just didn't have the same buzz about it when the victim had done you no wrong. There had been that girl from the nightclub out of town, she was only too willing to follow the charming gentleman back to his private quarters. He remembered how wowed the little thing had been at the obvious sign of wealth the villa displayed. The excited tourist, an English girl with a ghastly Liverpudlian accent couldn't stop gloating about how she'd landed herself a "rich one". Bobby only needed the tiniest slight to justify her untimely death. Torture had been much more arduous a task without the help of his former employees, in the early days he considered making contact with Lionel and Joe, Bobby's former henchmen. The problem was they were both serving long sentences thanks to him. That had also been one of the deals for his own freedom. The girl's drawn out end had taken him back to his more youthful days, improvisation with very limited resources. Whilst rifling through the previous inhabitants left over kitchen supplies, he found two packets of small watch batteries. He recalled watching a news program, warning parents to keep the acid filled tablets of death away from their young children. Apparently once dissolved in the stomach they could have lethal and painful effects. Patience hadn't been on his side however, after the first dose had been forced down her gullet, he'd grown bored of the screaming Liverpudlian accent and finished the girl off quickly opting for a less imaginative kitchen knife. He just couldn't get excited about it, the girl had nothing to confess to him. At least the young man who was visiting him today had some information that could be slowly extracted for a real purpose. Yes! It was true. Against all the odds, the what ifs – Bobby Cavendish had fallen in love again. It was this all-consuming obsession he called love that led to the decision to once again become his true self. The girl, he didn't know her name, had taken his breath away. Bobby had never known love before Emily but somehow, he knew this feeling was stronger still. The new girl, he'd find out her name if it killed him (or someone), picked fruit in the fields not far from his villa. At first, he was alarmed by someone in such close proximity to the private grounds but as he set out to protect his territory, it became abundantly clear that this is what people called love at first sight. Watching her from the exterior walls his mind was fed with oxytocin for the first time in five years without drugs. Bobby followed the creature sent from God himself, the girl begun to sing in her native tongue. Bobby had never heard something so beautiful in all his years. The melody flowed through every sixty thousand miles of his veins, an almost unbearable pleasure of need. She'd allowed him to follow as far as the mysterious monastery-come-orphanage then shyly turned towards him before running off into the religious grounds. Hard to get was it? Bobby had marvelled at the girl's mischievous nature. Well my dear, one is happy to play your game. That was two weeks ago, and Bobby had been busy since. First, he tried talking to the priest. After his experience with Emily, Bobby wasn't prepared to play the waiting game again. Apparently, the priest was as much of a primitive neanderthal as the rest of the villagers. The meeting didn't go to plan. Neither men could communicate properly so Bobby tried being patient, using basic words such as "girl" and "villa", but the priest only become more agitated. Bobby wanted to assure him that his intentions were pure and that he would be able to provide a good life for the girl. He used basic words again "me" "money" "girl" "good life" but this had only served to infuriate the religious man more. After some frustration and swallowed pride on Bobby's behalf he reluctantly returned to his villa. Ordinarily anyone who disrespected him as the priest did would already be in mortal agony, but this was his future father-in-law of sorts. Bobby knew when to offer respect. Following the altercation, he mulled over different ways to find out more about the girl. Oh, but for a name at least!

BEEP

BEEP

BEEP

Bobby snapped out of his daydream and turned off the alarm. Had it been twenty minutes already? No rest for the wicked, he mused standing up from the sun lounger.

He descended the stairs into the former wine cellar, Bobby stared at the young adult in the giant vat of liquid. The visibly distressed individual stared back with agonised eyes that popped from the skull. He moaned in terror through his gagged mouth. Bobby couldn't help noticing the victim's long hair had already turned peroxide blonde, submerged under the bleach.

"I don't know what you're moaning about, people pay a lot of money for hair like that these days." He laughed to no one. He did miss an audience. Bobby yanked the gag from the dying lad's mouth, "You have one chance. What is her name?"

"¡Por favor! ¡Por favor! ¡No me mates! ¡Por favor! No sé qué me estás diciendo. ¡Haré lo que quieras!" begged the young man.

"Well, don't say I didn't warn you!" Bobby bellowed as he opened a tap feeding the tank with more of the corrosive liquid. The man child shouted with increased panic in his own language. It became obvious that he had either no intention of handing over any information or, no idea what the mad man who'd kidnapped him and placed him into an oversized fish tank of bleach wanted. Considering this possibility, Bobby had an idea. He had a photo of the girl on his phone. There was no doubt that the lad knew the girl, Bobby had with much displeasure seen the two of them together. He'd been watching the object of his desire as usual, careful to keep a safe distance. It wouldn't do to approach her yet, there was so much more he needed to discover first. On top of that, he knew she felt the same way – he was only too happy to play her game. The way she'd seen him hiding behind a tree, choosing to run away in a flirtatious manner. The playful way she would look away when she saw him looking from the boundary to the monastery. Bobby enjoyed the game they shared, that was until she had been with this boy. Not even a man yet! But Bobby knew what she was doing. It was all part of the act – the chase. She was offering him this gift. Yes, that was what she was up to. She wanted Bobby to torture this poor fellow, to find out about her. This pathetic whelp probably had a crush on her – not that he could blame him for that. The girl was Pandora herself. It had been so obvious, when he approached them, the girl had pointed at Bobby and said something angrily to the boy before running off towards their home. The lad had been surprisingly strong – but Bobby Cavendish was stronger.

He turned back to the matter at hand, producing a mobile phone and unlocking the home screen to reveal the photo already on his background display. After taking another gasp at her beauty, Bobby showed the screen to the submerged boy.

"Who? Who this girl?" He did his best to keep it simple. The petrified native looked at the photo shaking his head. "No. No girl," he stammered.

"Girl! Yes! Fuck! Ing! Girl!" roared Bobby. He really thought the photo had been enough. It looked like they were getting somewhere. Apparently not. Bobby opened the tap feeding the tank, the level of bleach was rapidly rising and lapped at the prisoner's lips. Soon it would become too much and wouldn't take long for the liquid to enter his mouth.

"Estela! Estela! Por favor, no la lastimes. ¡Por favor, déjame ir!"

Estela! Finally, he had a name. Bobby's legs trembled, a giddy dizziness almost taking him off his feet. The joy, he could see it now. Bobby and Estela. Estela and Bobby. It was really going to happen this time. It wouldn't be easy: he'd probably have to learn her language or even better they could move somewhere else. He was done with this heat, maybe Canada would be nice? But something felt wrong, there was something Bobby was forgetting. It wasn't the almost depleted supply of money, although that was a concern. Nor was it for any worry of blowing Hargreaves' whereabouts – he had too much on Phipps. But there was something…

"Guurgh...g..g p.. Por favor…Dejar…me...guuu…"

The fluid level rose so high that the victim was currently standing on tip toes. It was too late for him now. Disinterestedly, Bobby made his way back upstairs. What was it that he'd forgotten? … It wasn't until he was half away across the kitchen that it came to him… EMILY!

A Good Start

Life on cold cases had become much to Austin's surprise a step in the right direction, not just for his career. The 'office' he'd been relocated to hadn't seen a decorator since the nineteen seventies when the building was opened, the industrial sized pipework ran through, disappearing off to heat the upper floors, a constant reminder, that this was the basement. The one tiny window, above head height, stained brown from smoke. The Yeovil police department was in dire need of refurbishment and plans were in place for a four-million-pound overhaul, such was the 'current state of the building'. Despite the conditions, Austin found his sunshine elsewhere – Julie Richardson. He'd first met Julie when signing out his first (ever) set of case files. She was the person responsible for signing them over to him. Austin had been his usual painfully awkward self, around beautiful women, or any woman, to be accurate. His eyes had nervously flickered towards her as she looked down to the files, allowing him to take in her glorious frames. Never had Austin seen such a beautiful pair of glasses. The way they magnified her brown eyes! The way they then both quickly pulled their hands away when they touched the file at the same time, his hand brushing over Julie's for a brief moment. He took a moment to see, well, working cold cases didn't seem too bad.

Hours of being placed on hold and listening to endless classical music had finally rewarded Austin with some information on the car. A Lexus registered to Paul Hargreaves never had an insurance claim against it, nor was it even reported as stolen. Austin could only assume that it was the former sergeant who disposed of the car at that scrap yard in the village of Colney. Had he been getting rid of evidence because of the earlier events in the day? There was one thing clear to Austin – Sergeant Paul Hargreaves was a bent cop – was this the big break he'd been looking for? This could be the case that he exalted to Internal-Investigation-Division's attention! Who would have thought an act of discipline from Carl Bragg could actually set Austin on his chosen path?!

Austin had organised the day for making phone calls with the DVLA and insurance companies. The scrap yard where the vehicle had been disposed of hadn't been helpful. The receptionist laughed at him, just for asking if anyone could remember the Man who scrapped the Lexus five years before.

"If I remembered every Tom, Dick and Harry who dumped a car off I wouldn't be working here would I?" She didn't hide the sarcasm. Austin wondered if she would be so rude in person and might it be worth a visit to look at their records? All scrapyards were now required to take an address and a proof of identification from customers. Thus, he decided to push the woman for more information.

"Madam, are you telling me that you have a lot of practically brand new and expensive cars brought to you by police officers? Surely, you would remember something about that?"

"I'm not the only one who works here, Mister... although sometimes I wonder, lazy buggers my husband employs, none of them stay here that long and if it definitely was any of them then you'd be out of luck."

"What about your husband? Can I speak to him?"

"I'll take your name and number, but he's always ever so busy."

"Madam, can I remind you this is a police investigation. The matter is of high importance."

"Oh, is it? Well why didn't you say? Who are you anyway? Morris Minor or something was it? Don't recognise that name, we've got our own police force down here you know."

Yes, Austin did know, not that you'd think so. He hadn't been able to contact the Colney police branch either by phone or email. If he could have talked to a fellow officer about his enquiries, then he most certainly would choose them over the infuriating woman currently on the phone.

"My name is Detective Constable Austin Healey, Madam and I would greatly appreciate it if your husband could call me back as soon as possible."

"Austin Healey? Wasn't that a bloody car? Pretty sure my husband had a few of them come through here back in the day," she chortled to herself. Austin was used to a lifetime of ridicule due to his car enthusiast father's attempt at a funny name. The Austin Healey, by no way considered a bad car couldn't be regarded as a great car either. How he'd longed for a commonly mundane moniker such as David, John, James or just anything that wasn't as attention seeking as his own. He finished the conversation making sure to check she'd taken all his contact numbers, email and even the Yeovil Police department's address. He didn't want to miss the scrap yard owner, there was clearly something strange going on regarding Paul Hargreaves' last recorded activities. Austin would find it hard to believe that the owner wouldn't remember such a car. He'd just have to wait until Mrs McKay had passed the note on to her husband, if she did. In the meantime, a visit to Sergeant Hargreaves might be in order, Austin had checked – Mr Hargreaves' – file. There was an address in London but when he'd tried the landline associated, a woman answered. This pleasant-sounding lady informed Austin they bought the house a few years before and confirmed Paul Hargreaves as the previous owner. The lady explained they had never met, as everything was done through broker. They didn't have a forwarding address either and so Austin turned his attentions to the allusive sergeant's police file. By the age of thirty, Paul Hargreaves had in fact been a Detective Inspector, something Austin himself, now knocking on the door of the big three-oh, dreamed of. Austin who hadn't even made sergeant yet, could only imagine how someone with as dark a cloud as Hargreaves had so rapidly progressed. After this clearly impressive career on paper, there was a void. Two weeks short of three years to be precise and not a single record of that period. After that it just showed Sergeant Paul Hargreaves on medical leave. There was no mention of the obvious demotion in rank. Nor was there any regarding his medical condition, although both would have needed special authorisation from a superior. The records showed no updates from the last five years. Presumably the sergeant was still on the sick. Human resources seemed hell bent on kicking employees out with so much as a couple days off in a year for anything these days. Austin had never known such untold and fostered leniency allowed to anyone from the much revered and callous HR department. So why Hargreaves? Before he asked Chief Superintendent Bragg for clearance on the files, there was another phone call to make. Hargreaves' last job role had been in Bristol, the leading man there at the time was Chief

Constable Phipps. An officer of the law who Austin had admired greatly over the years, albeit from afar. The man had almost singlehandedly destroyed organised crime in the Bristol area some years ago. Austin held great admiration for him. Phipps made promotion from Chief Superintendent for his part, and as Chief Constable of 'Avon and Somerset Police' he incorporated Austin's department of Yeovil. Surely it wouldn't hurt to give the highly decorated man a call would it? Phipps had been Hargreaves' superior at the last time in active duty so if anyone knew anything about the mysterious Hargreaves then it would be him. Austin would make the call, but first, the anxious excitement via Julie's desk to return her files. He hoped that after being taken 'off guard' in their first encounter he would be better prepared this time.

Jules

Words reached her of Austin's reassignment, before his first day in

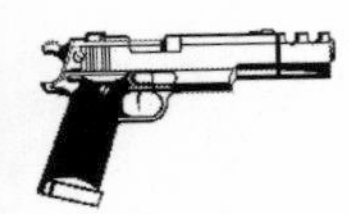

the basement office. Jules couldn't believe her luck – the man was a legend in the bird watching community. Many a late night she'd spent reading Austin's tantalising blogs on the Birder's website. The group also allowed registered members to discuss their own sightings through a message board. The nights had been filled with their dialogue, although Austin would only have known her by her online handle, MissSparrowhawk87. Julie had considered many a time whether to divulge her real name to the celebrated Birder, fear of rejection put a stop to that. It may have helped to ease their awkward encounter when he'd first come to sign out the case files. On the other hand, it may have proved too much for MissSparrowhawk87's nerves. Her keyboard relationship had spanned countless hours. Rarely had they reluctantly ended their chats without both feeling there was so much more they could go on discussing. When Austin Healey appeared kitten-like in her department that morning, the atmosphere between them as two lovestruck teens, hiding behind acne with their shortened smiles. It was all she could do to keep a professional element – forcing herself to make eye contact. Austin wasn't what many women would consider handsome. He was short compared to his fellow officers, thinning hair and glasses sized too big, curiously appearing older than his years – that tight rump though! Clearly, he was a man who kept himself in shape. Julie certainly didn't rate herself highly by any means despite her mother and a handful of friends telling her otherwise, she just didn't see it. Gangly arms and long legs – repulsive. Coupled with the sharp angles in her face offered little confidence whilst looking in the mirror. In truth, under the baggy jumpers and loose-fitting jeans hid a body that would be the envy of many a woman. Little did she know Austin found her the most beautiful person on the planet. Finding out she was the fascinating MissSparrowhawk87 may have pushed him over the edge. Julie or "Jules" to her few friends and family, had contemplated hitting the 'get friend' button on the popular social media platform. At one time, emboldened by a few glasses of red wine on a Friday evening, she'd sent the request. Instantly Jules had been overwhelmed with panic and remorse and quickly hit the button cancelling the request and hoping beyond all measures that the other user wouldn't see the notification. Their bumbling first meeting had changed everything, now she had an excuse to request him and properly this time… she would definitely do it… nothing was going to stop her… but later… probably… as long as nothing came up.

Something did come up, or someone at least. As Jules looked up from the thumbnail of Austin on her phone, she saw a person's silhouette standing on the other side of her internal office windows. Whoever was standing there clearly didn't realise that she could see their shadow through the metal blinds. They came up towards the door before stopping abruptly, walking away again and then seemed to change their mind, repeating the process perhaps three or four times.

"Hello?" Jules called out sheepishly, "Can I help you?"

"Oh… Oh s s sorry. It's just me… I mean, sorry. Erm, its Austin. Detective Constable Austin Healy." Austin still stood just outside the office door. Could he be as nervous as her? It wouldn't have crossed her mind that he liked her.

"Hello Detective, would you like to come in?"

"Oh, yes… I mean yes thank you. Erm…" Austin shuffled into the office and approached Jules' desk.

"Julie."

"I beg your pardon?" Austin asked puzzled.

What an idiot she was, she had been sure he had forgotten her name so in her nerves offered it to him again. "My name, Detective… It's Julie but everyone calls me Jules… well not everyone obviously, I don't really know a lot of people. Well… obviously there's a lot of people who work in this building, but I don't really know them well enough but… erm… you can call me Jules if you like?" For God's sake why wouldn't she just shut up? Unable to stop the verbal diarrhoea cascading from her mouth.

Austintatious

He couldn't believe it! within seconds he'd already embarrassed himself. Jules'd obviously been repeating her name to him – as if he could forget – Austin just hadn't expected her to be so forthcoming and hadn't the time to prepare himself. So confident too! He'd barely been able to keep up with what she was saying, but every syllable bounced around the inside of his head like an exotic bird testing the boundaries of its cage. Quickly! He needed to make a comeback and fast, but instead, just stood firmly rooted to the spot. His brain unable to send instructions to static vocal cords. The colour in his cheeks brightened as he became increasingly aware of the growing silence. Her alluring eyes stared patiently back at him, his own darted between the floor and the ceiling. If he didn't say anything soon then it would become irreparably uncomfortable to do anything but leave. That's when he remembered the box of files in his arms. Suddenly, involuntary words blurted out of him.

"Case files. Erm. Thanks…" As he placed the files down Austin noticed a photograph on Jules desk. "Oooh, nice tit...willow. Tit… sorry I mean…" He trailed off sensing the damage was already done.

Dirty pictures

Jules cursed herself for causing the unbearable atmosphere they found themselves in. It had all looked lost when he left the files, that was until she watched his eyes lock onto her photo. The picture was her pride and joy. The Willow Tit – a beautiful little bird whose numbers had plummeted in recent years. It had been a great achievement capturing it through her camera lens and now the birdwatching community's equivalent of Lewis Hamilton was commenting on it.

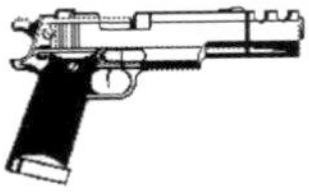

"Thank you! I'm so proud of it. I mean it took me forever to take it, I'd almost given up all hope in finding it to be honest. My friends thought I was crazy, you know, staying in the woods on my own and everything, but it was so worth it. She was beautiful, I can't believe there hasn't been more done to protect them. Such a graceful bird…"

Love birds

Austin was hypnotised by Jules, studying every perfect contour of her facial structure. He'd lost track of what she was saying, his mind running around in circles as his belly flip-flopped. Women like this didn't commit their free time to painstaking hours of waiting for rare birds. At least not the ones he'd always known. Could it actually be true? Was this angel sent from heaven really a bird enthusiast? Austin had to know. He might be shit with women, but he knew his birds!

Jules

...and that's when I saw that she had a nest with two eggs waiting to hatch! Against all the odds too. It was just..." she trailed off realising that Austin's eyes were glazed over. You stupid girl! He's probably heard it all before, she fumed at herself. His eyes seemed to refocus as she finished her sentence, "...perfect."

Austin

Yes! Here it comes. Austin was ready, he knew exactly what to say. Only recently he'd written a blog about the Willow Tit. There couldn't be a better conversation starter. For now he was just enjoying the rapture of her voice, but he was ready. Here it goes...

"…and that's when I saw that she had a nest with two eggs waiting to hatch! Against all the odds too. It was just…"

Was this it? This was definitely it. Had she actually finished talking or had she just asked him a question? Why the hell hadn't he been listening to her?

"…perfect."

Perfect? What had been perfect? Suddenly Austin couldn't even remember what day it was, let alone what he was going to say. Something about birds, his mind was blindly fumbling for anything. In the end he kept it simple, there was always tomorrow.

"Thank you for the files… it's nice to have met you. See you tomorrow?" For Austin it was at least not too bad. Ok, he had failed to respond to anything the girl had been trying to talk to him about but at least he managed to string some coherent words together.

"Oh, sorry yes. Yes, nice to meet you too Detective Constable Healey."

If Austin's feet were touching the floor, then he certainly didn't feel them as he floated towards the exit. Hearing her speak his name had given him a rare surge of confidence and before he could stop himself, he turned back.

"Call me Austin… Jules."

Old Habits

It had taken a great deal of effort and `communal' wine to calm the girl for Alvaro to extract her story. Before he could, Alvaro cleaned the dried blood from a nasty cut on her head. Between the heaving sobs and painful wincing from the antiseptic, she'd managed to relay most of the details regarding Diego's abduction. Regardless of his best advice, Estela and her love had visited the fruit trees in the loco man's territory. Alvaro knew how strong-willed Diego could be and didn't doubt for a second that the visit had been the headstrong lad's way of warning the man off. Love could embolden the weakest of men and Diego was anything but. Regardless of the reason for encroaching upon the stranger's property, Alvaro saw no reason to disbelieve Estela's recounting of the last time she'd seen Diego.

"He was just standing there behind a tree Padre! Like a stalker, he came out from nowhere. The look in his eyes made me feel sick, nobody has looked at me like that… since..." she broke off to stifle the tears before composing herself with another sip of the wine, "I know what men like him want. But Diego flew straight at him, threatening the man to stay away from us. I tried to shout for him to come with me, to just run away, but he… he wouldn't listen and that's when the man hit him." Estela this time unable to keep herself from crying, the recollection of the incident proving too much.

Alvaro cursed the boy, he cursed himself for not acting sooner and warning the man off, but most of all he cursed the loco man. He'd hoped to keep his past behind him, but it was inevitable. The experience from his former life would be required.

"Estela, it's ok. You haven't been back long yourself, Diego could still come through that door any minute now."

"No Padre… I don't think he will. After I finished running back to the monastery, I knew you would be too angry with us for going against your wishes, so I returned to the villa by myself."

Alvaro groaned, "Estela I might have been angry with you, but your safety is paramount to me. You too could have been hurt. Tell me child, what happened when you went back?"

"I know Padre, I've been so stupid. I thought that I could reason with the man myself but when I returned to the spot where Diego had been struck down, I could find neither of them. I did my best to remain silent and prowled the outer walls of the villa. I finally found a spot where the mortar in the stone wall allowed me to peak through to the swimming pool area. The loco man was there, relaxing on a sunbed as if nothing had happened. I watched him for some time before he went back inside. There was no sign of Diego, so I found a part of the wall that looked climbable, digging my feet into the cracks I began to pull myself up. I could feel the top of the wall with my hand and that's when I lost my footing. The next thing I knew, my head was thumping with agony and the sun had left the sky. That's when I made my way back to you. I'm so sorry Padre," she broke off into a crescendo of wailing tears.

"Don't be sorry Estela. Diego may be ok, perhaps he is somewhere in town massaging his bruised ego." Although Alvaro very much doubted it. This man's sanity was clearly an issue to take into consideration.

"Diego's a strong boy in his prime. I am of a similar age to the loco man and I don't think I would come off better against Diego in a fight."

"No Padre, you don't understand. The loco man didn't hit him with his hands. He hit Diego with a gun."

Old habits never die hard, Alvaro had already stood up and collected his long-ago retired revolver from its hiding place. He closed the desk drawer, slid one of the two clips into the gun and pocketed the other before putting the holster on his belt. Alvaro's senses came back to him long enough to notice the wide-eyed look coming from Estela.

"Padre?" she uttered, "What are you doing?"

"Estela, I need you to stay here. I will be back soon I promise. I need you to look after the children." He headed to the front door, pulling on his jacket to cover the gun.

"But Padre, why do you have a gun? Surely we should just call the police?"

"I need you to trust me child. Even if we could call the police, it would take them far too long to get here. I should have talked to you and Diego sooner. I know that now, but I will tell you everything when I get back… with Diego." He left through the heavy wooden door, closing it on the questioning face of Estela. Alvaro hoping it wouldn't be the last time he saw her.

Hard Labour

There were many things Bobby missed about his former life but  disposing of human cadavers wasn't one of them. He found himself having an increasing respect for Lionel and Joe – his former henchmen. There was no fun to be had in dragging a dead weight around, digging holes or even worse, burning the bodies. The foul smell they emitted gave him no satisfaction. It was this arduous clean up job which he supposed had led to some of the joy being drained from his favourite past time. Staring at the young male floating in the tank of bleach, Bobby considered leaving the body to see if the chemical would do the job for him – if it would at all. Leaving it to chance that someone could come snooping about was way too risky. What if Estela – his heart fluttered – came looking for him again? She was an inquisitive creature after all, he mused. Hadn't she been the one to seek him out at the villa on numerous occasions? In truth, no she hadn't. Estela wasn't unusually inquisitive at all – in fact, it was safe to say that she was less so than most people. The only reason she'd been so close to Bobby's villa in the first place was for the ripe apple trees. She'd only been to the area twice. With the lack of any real social contact, the Spanish heat and Bobby's already fragmented grasp on sanity (not that he saw it that way), Estela wanted him just as much as he did her. With that in mind, Bobby drained the tank, put on some rather fetching yellow marigolds and moved the body.

He dragged the corpse into a corner of the basement where the cement flooring had long ago crumbled. Bobby found he could move the larger pieces without too much exertion, he was still a fit man – physically at least. After clearing what he hoped was a big enough opening, he dragged the body over. It would have to do, he decided. The basement had some tools hanging on one side where he selected a shovel and began digging. After barely a foot deep he decided that was enough exercise for one day. It was funny really; Bobby Cavendish was brilliant at the killing part, but even he could admit that his disposal techniques were shit. He shoved the deceased Diego into the shallow grave and threw enough dirt to cover the boy's features before piling the fragments of hardcore back on top. It was crude, but already late in the evening now and Bobby had to pack. He was going on holiday!

Ambiel Music

Before he left the office, Austin passed his message to a member of staff at the Avon and Somerset headquarters in Portishead. Chief Constable Phipps had been unavailable as he had matters to address in Bristol. The helpful clerk had assured Austin the message would be delivered. Despite the woman's friendly manner, he decided against including the exact nature of the call. He nearly left out Paul Hargreaves' name. There was every possibility that the long absence could be due to a sensitive and personal nature. Austin had even considered the police officer in question could be working undercover, that didn't fit in with the demotion in rank though. With the day done, he headed out to the car park to pick up his little Toyota only to be greeted by smeared shit over his front window. By the characteristic scent he deduced that it was at least not human. Cleaning a dog turd from the windscreen didn't faze him, what did was the brazen act being carried out in a police station car park that was monitored by CCTV. Could the perpetrators be more blatant? Apparently, they could.

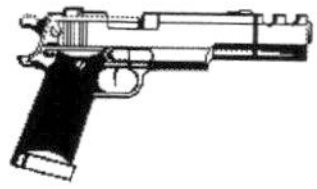

"Oi! Dustbin Healy, how do you like your new office in the basement?" One of the passing uniformed Officers laughed. The other joined in sensing an opportunity to kick a man when he was already down, "You fucking grass!" Seeing that his colleague hadn't heard enough to laugh, the man stammered out a further insult in the hope of winning the other man's respect, "You fucking... shit… cunt!" This tickled the officers who sensing the fun had passed, moved on, pleased with the dressing down they administered. Austin had already memorised both men's numbers and would be requesting all surveillance tapes first thing Monday morning. He was in too good a mood to let it worry him tonight. Julie or Jules and their first proper conversation had given him too much delight to dwell on such matters as a bit of shit smearing. Besides, Austin had become used to such occurrences. There was also the anticipation of receiving a call from the highly decorated Chief Constable Phipps, he couldn't help but hope the more experienced man may even put in a good word for him to internal affairs. For now, that was all just fantasy.

Today was Friday, so Austin treated himself to a pint can of Guinness. He closed the fridge and made his way – two steps – to the living room. Leaving the cloudy liquid to settle, he checked all his messages in the unlikely hope that Phipps had called. He wasn't surprised to find them empty, but still it did nothing to sour his mood. Austin's heart was pounding every time he let his mind slip back to her – Jules – it was all he could do to stop himself from searching for her on a popular social media platform. He had no doubts he would find her, after all, Austin was a very thorough detective. Morally, it troubled him, however. Would that make him a stalker? But then what were people really doing on dating websites?

He'd never been brave enough to try but Austin had an understanding in how they worked. People making up their minds about a complete stranger before they'd ever met them. Swipe left, swipe right. Either way, he had to busy his mind, so he turned on the laptop. There was unfinished work to do on his current blog, a fine piece about the Spotted Flycatcher but Austin's mind kept straying back to Jules. He thought maybe some music would help him focus, even just for a little bit. For all his faults, Austin had a fantastic taste in music. He opened his music account and searched artists for Man from Reno and selected the track 'Moses'. The dirty distortion of the first guitar cut out a riff before the harmonic notes of the second joined in. The riff repeated as the bass and drums came crashing down to join the affray. It was a melodic wall of sound. Austin was momentarily taken away to a place where nothing else much mattered, the dirty rock music allowing him to free his anxieties. Without realising it, Austin had finished the Guinness. Well, it was a special occasion. One more wouldn't hurt. Would it?

Austin poured out the second can as the band's B-side began to play. It was titled 'Never gonna get it', the story of his life. It didn't stop him from dancing some more and when they finished, Austin put on another band he loved, Fu Manchu. Halfway through the third drink an unusual sense of mischievousness had come across him. The logo for the social media App was just there on the screen. Surely it could do no harm. Maybe just a quick search. She might not even have a page, Austin reasoned with himself. If that was the case then it wouldn't be a problem, perhaps then he could put it all to rest until Monday. Yes. He would just check to see if she was on there, there was nothing wrong with that…

Ten minutes later and everything had gone wrong! There was no problem locating Julie Richardson from Yeovil. From the list of names, he'd known straightaway the right one. Her profile picture gave it all away, displaying the same photo of the Willow Tit that sat on her desk. Innocently, Austin had clicked on the profile and searched through her page. Non surprisingly as a member of the police, Jules had set her profile to private. It gave little away, but Austin saw all he needed. A handful of profile pictures showing her out with friends, equally beautiful in each one, but it was the last picture that stole the air from his lungs. In this picture, Jules was standing in a striking pose (hopefully taken by one of her girlfriends! Oh my! He hadn't even considered a boyfriend until now) modelling the latest Ghillie suit. She made it look sexy! The all in one suit that resembled a onesie covered in leaves and twigs made Austin come over all out of sorts. The guilt he suffered from the growing bulge in his budgie smugglers caused him a sudden alarm to close the page down. He would not disrespect her like this! Unfortunately, in his haste to shut the page, Austin hit the friend request button. He watched in horror as the icon changed to a tick. What have I done? In a panicked reflex he quickly hit the cursor on the request button again to cancel the request, the screen changed back to 'add friend'. Apparently, he had hit it too many times though as the computer played catch up with his over excited fingers the screen flicked back and forth between 'get friend' and 'request pending'. Eventually it rested back on 'get friend' so Austin took his time and closed down the computer, not wanting to leave any more risk. It had been close, but he was pretty sure he'd escaped what could have been a very embarrassing situation come Monday morning. Deciding that he'd had enough excitement for one day and not trusting the amount of alcohol he'd consumed, Austin decided to call it a night and head for bed. It was just as he was close to slipping into dreamland that a nagging thought began to plague him – do people receive notifications even if the other person rescinds the request?

Top Brass

The small white pitted ball snaked along the smooth grass of the green. Chief Constable Phipps could already see it would never make it to the hole, the trajectory had been off from the moment it left his putter.

"You're losing your touch Alan. Ten years ago, you'd have made that look easy." Alan Phipps and Richard Mason had been playing golf with each other for over twenty years. Phipps had still not grown to love Mason's relentless jibes. "We're all getting older Richard," he replied. Richard Mason held the role of police and crime commissioner and the friendship, a common bond over the love of golf, had always benefitted Phipps. As Richard Mason climbed the ladder, Alan Phipps followed a few rungs behind. In exchange, Mason always knew he had a man he could call on. Neither were spring chickens anymore, so those times were mostly behind them. Between them holding the two highest positions in the force, they had arrived at the top table.

"Steady on Phipps, you're not that far behind me. Talking of which, what was this retirement bullshit you mentioned?"

"Not retirement exactly just a little relocation. I see it as more of a sidestep, out of the spotlight but still ready to provide my skills if you so need them… Sir." Phipps wasn't ready to retire his badge yet, but a good opportunity had become available and things weren't getting any easier these days. Cormac McCarthy couldn't have summed it up any better, this really was No Country For Old Men. Since the removal of Bobby Cavendish's empire of which had done wonders for Phipps' career, a new breed of criminal had emerged. The gangs who now controlled the streets had proven to be almost impenetrable. There was just no code of honour, the whole thing had become overrun by highly sensitive and hormonal teens. At least Bobby Cavendish had manners. He'd demanded respect but also kept the streets safer. Criminals who had stepped out of line were either dealt with by Bobby or, handed over to the police as part of an 'exchange' that suited both parties. The new guard lacked any level of respect for anything other than their own pride. They all thought they were 'Bobby from the Bronx' – Phipps was done with all that.

Mason's phone started ringing in his pocket, when he answered it Phipps finished his short putt, finally putting the ball in the hole. He bent down to retrieve it and returned his club to the bag whilst Mason finished an obviously heated argument with his wife.

"That bloody kid of mine. School's only found out he's been knocking out pills to pupils. You're lucky you never had any Alan. Come see me after the weekend, we'll look into this retirement plan or whatever you want to call it. Sounds like I might need you to pull some strings for me as it is, depending on this meeting with the school. See you later Alan." Mason moved off towards the club house already back on his phone. There was a couple more holes left so Phipps thought it would be rude not to finish up.

After a very successful eighteenth hole – typical that Mason wasn't around to witness his glory – Phipps headed back to his car and called his office for any messages. The only one of interest came from a Detective Constable Austin Healey. Phipps thought it must be a mistake, the admin assured him that was the name given. He would have dismissed the message entirely, but an enquiry into one of his former officers had peaked Phipps' interest. He'd have a look into this Austin Healey and find out who his superior was. Phipps didn't like people sniffing around his staff – especially deceased ones.

Bird Catcher

The squat Toyota Yaris hurtled towards Yeovil Police headquarters

at a risky thirty-two miles an hour. Emboldened by Golden Earring's 'Radar Love' blasting through the speakers, Austin could not wait to get to work. Waking up on Saturday morning with an incredibly rare hangover, he recalled his actions the previous night. The unknown consequences of his fumbling fingers on Jules' profile had cast a dark cloud over the rest of the weekend. So much so, Austin cancelled his plans to attend the monthly miniature railway meeting. His racing mind hadn't let him concentrate in the slightest on his unfinished blogs, they usually engrossed him with hours of uninterrupted entertainment. Austin just couldn't shake the scenario of Monday morning from his head, playing out multiple eventualities over and over until he wanted to scream. What if Jules did receive the request and told everyone at work about it. He could imagine her laughing in the canteen with the other officers who would take nothing but pleasure in his humiliation. But then something even more unexpected happened and Austin was on cloud nine. Jules had sent him a request! At first, he was certain it was a joke. Had one of the above colleagues found out about his crush and set up a fake profile in order to ridicule him? He'd seen from previous cases how easy it was to steal someone's identity. But no, it just didn't add up and her profile had too many personal details, and pictures, to be faked. It hadn't stopped him from fretting over accepting the request though. No. Austin stared at the screen for another two hours before finally hitting accept. He'd been slightly disappointed in the anti-climax of the moment, that was until he realised that Jules profile, now open to him with "friend" status, allowed him to see more that was previously hidden. Austin spent a great deal of time reading every status Jules had shared and their adjoining comments. He felt like he knew her better already. It turned out they were in some mutual groups together, mostly related to a shared love of birds. The extra insight had done little to settle his newfound feelings for the woman. The more he discovered about her, the more impossible it seemed that she would ever be interested in him. Jules was perfect. She even spent some of her own time volunteering to catch speeding motorists in high accident rural villages. Jules was also a member of her neighbourhood watch and set up a speed awareness campaign in her own village. A woman after his own heart, but was Austin her's? No, probably not. Everyone was at it these days, friend requesting friends' friends of friends and so and so on. It wasn't that common for him however and so made it that bit more special.

Austin searched the police quarters' car park for a bay directly under a CCTV camera – he hadn't forgotten about the dog shit. As he got out of the car, two uniformed officers, not the same as the previous pair walked past smirking. Austin recognised one of the men, Darren Somerville.

He and Darren had trained together when they first joined the force and struck up an unlikely friendship. Darren being the typical likely lad, popular with girls, likes drinking and bantering with the lads. Austin was… well Austin… he was the polar opposite. For the first time in Austin's adult life he had a friend, Darren looked out for him. On the times he could brave it, Austin would go to the pub favoured by the local police force. When other colleagues would predictably pick on Austin's weaknesses (something he had grown accustomed to and why he avoided such social gatherings), Darren would always be straight in there with a witty retort to silence the offender. Not only that, he had this way of turning it into praise for Austin. Other people in the force began to respect him more, finally he'd found a place where he belonged. But it all came to an end when he realised Darren was using him all along.

Austin knew from early on in life that he was destined for a career in the police force. His parents had seen the signs too and despite their best efforts to steer him towards a different vocation, Austin prevailed. It wasn't that Mr and Mrs Healey disliked the police or doubted their only child's suitability for the role, but as two weed smoking parents it was closer than they would like to be to the Law. Young Austin would bound up to every officer he saw to ask questions and swear his allegiance to his future employers. Meanwhile Mr and Mrs Healey would shuffle uncomfortably up behind him making paranoid small talk with the officers. Things had got even worse by the time Austin reached his teens. He became aware of drug abuse via fellow students and the school's prehistoric scare mongering. It wasn't long until Austin put together the strange smells and paraphernalia that his parents tried to keep hidden from him. At first, he'd been confused, surely it couldn't be. Both parents worked full time professional jobs, they always provided him with everything he ever needed. The picture was all wrong, everything that the school, TV and society educated him was that drug abusers were bad. That was when Austin made the decision to investigate. It hadn't taken much; he really was becoming quite the detective. Whereas the other boys in his school year were putting their efforts into chasing girls and stealing booze from their parents, Austin used his time to investigate wrong doings in his school. The perpetrators of these minor school yard misdemeanours didn't take kindly to his own love of justice. Much to his bemusement, the teachers didn't react in the way Austin would have expected. Instead of receiving praise for his valiant efforts he usually found himself chastised for being a tattletale. This wasn't helped by his inability to exclude his educators from investigation. By the time he finished high school, Austin found his only friend was the headmaster – a former police officer, who himself had left the force due to the corruption he'd endured. And so, it was after staking out his own parents one night, having led them to believe he was attending a friend's sleepover (an unlikely story by all accounts) –

that he witnessed both parents in the act of smoking one of them druggie spliffs! He confronted the giggling and red-eyed pair there and then. Mr and Mrs Healey refused to stop their extra-curricular activities and their relationship with young Austin grew ever more distant from there on in. Perhaps it was best that once Austin enrolled himself into the police training programme, they helped buy him a flat. The Healey's had both retired early and shortly after Austin moved out, the couple sold their house, bought a VW camper and travelled around Europe. Sadly, he'd had very little contact with them since, aside from the annual birthday or Christmas card. It was for the best.

Austin had grown accustomed to his own company and didn't resent his parents, but Darren Somerville had shown him that perhaps having a friend wasn't such a bad thing after all. That was until Darren had shown his true colours.

The two of them had completed police officer training together and made the rank of constable. They'd even been lucky enough to join the same department and therefore continue their friendship, until Austin learned Darren was gleaming information from him to pass to a local small-time wannabe gangster. At first Austin was hurt by the way his only friend used him, but that was soon replaced with anger. An anger that was fuelled by his civic duty to report Darren. Much to Austin's surprise, instead of being removed from the force and even see jail time for perverting justice, Darren was merely moved on to a different department. In a bid to divert Austin's attention, his superior suggested he take the detective exam. Austin was ashamed to admit that the dangling carrot was enough for him to forget about Darren Somerville. That was until Darren had recently been reassigned back to Yeovil police department. Austin went straight to Chief Superintendent Bragg who told him to drop it for his own good. When Austin pushed his super for a reason of Darren's apparent immunity from the law, Bragg's reply was simple – "Don't fucking mess with the Mason's, Healey!"

But Darren Somerville wasn't going to ruin his good mood! Austin walked with what he believed was a "swagger", in all truth, he looked like he was dragging a dead leg. At least he was confident. Good effort Austin. Fortunately, he second guessed his new walk by the time he entered the building and made his way to the basement. He didn't walk as much as float, the mix of excitement and nerves making him lightheaded. He'd almost forgotten about the dog poo incident from Friday. He took a moment to consider leaving it until later or heading straight down to see Jules, but nerves soon made up his mind. Chief Superintendent Bragg it was. Austin knocked on the chief's door but there was no reply. A senior officer Austin knew by face walked past.

“Looking for Bragg? He’s not in today. Anything I can help you with Constable?”

Austin didn’t want to tell the officer he barely knew about the surveillance tapes. He might be in on it. He couldn’t trust anyone.

“No, thank you. Sir.” Austin turned and headed back towards the basement.

“Know any good car washes?” the officer laughed as he walked away.

It didn’t bother Austin – he’d put it off enough already. It was time to see Jules.

Indecent Exposure

After the fiasco of Friday, Jules had gone to visit her parents for the weekend. Despite owning her own modest flat, Jules loved returning to the family home. They'd always been very close; her father Brian had been a hard-working company man but was now retired and only too happy to see his only child. Jules' mum Pam doted upon her baby girl and would do anything for her. Jules knew she could talk to her mum about anything. So, she found herself eating home baked peanut butter cookies on her parent's couch.

"Mum I made a complete idiot of myself. It was awful."

"Jules love it sounds like he's a bit nervous himself," Pam reassured her daughter.

"But he's a detective! And a good one, not to mention his reputation in the Birder community. He's probably just being polite. Oh, the stupid rubbish I spluttered out."

"Any man would be lucky to be with my Julie," Jules dad added.

"Thanks Dad. But seriously he's a big deal."

"Why don't you find him on that Facepage thing dear? That's worked wonders for me finding some of my old friends. Everyone's on it these days!"

"Not bloody me," objected Brian.

"No, not you love. God forbid you should embrace modern technology. But what about it, Jules?"

"I don't know Mum. He is on there, I mean his profile is, but it would be so awkward on Monday if he didn't accept my request. Even if he did, I'd feel so desperate."

"Nonsense! Have you seen what the girls are like on that lust island show? That's desperate dear, not an innocent friend request."

"You and your bloody TV shows," Brian mumbled.

"You can shut up. I see your eyes light up at those girls in their swimsuits." Jules and her mum laughed as Brian played out mock disbelief.

"Okay. I'll think about it, but not tonight." Yeah, she would think about it. Out of habit she checked her phone, there was one notification. Could it be? When she clicked to see who it was it didn't show anyone. Strange.

XXX

Jules returned from her parents' house on Sunday afternoon and headed to her flat block, she was in for an unwanted surprise. Standing outside the security doors was a sweaty looking man wearing a no branded all in one tracksuit.

"Jules! I was beginning to think you were never coming home. I've been standing out here all day mad with worry. You haven't been home since Friday!"

"What are you doing here Gary? I asked you not come to my home anymore."

"I thought you told me not to call your phone anymore?"

"Both Gary, both. Please leave me alone I warned you I will get a restraining order if you don't stay away."

"Jules, I don't understand why you say these things? I know you don't really mean it. What have I done to make you want to hurt me this way?"

"Gary I'm not interested in you. I'm sorry but I never will be, and no amount of heavily breathing phone calls will change that. Neither will these uninvited visits to my home, nothing will Gary. It's not going to happen in a million years!"

"So, you're saying there is a chance?"

"No! Gary just go away!"

"But I found this beautiful Hawfinch nest for you, I can take you to it if you like."

Jules made her way to the entrance and attempted to sidestep around the stalker, but he intentionally moved into her way, lightly rubbing his groin on her thigh.

"Gary fuck off! I've got a boyfriend, he's a really hard detective so if I was you, I'd get out of here before he turns up."

Gary backed off visually hurt by Jules announcement. He was crushed inside; the sweaty little man had no idea that Jules was telling a bit of a porky.

"What do you mean? Does he know about us?" Gary stammered in disbelief.

"There is no us Gary. Now go!" Jules let herself into the building opening the door narrowly as possible, not wanting to give the stalker an inch. She shut the glass door on an immobile Gary and headed to the lift.

Jules had met her admirer at an annual birder meeting last year, Gary had wasted little time introducing himself. Even with Jules naivety she had noticed the number of heads turn her way when she entered the room and headed to the bar. It helped that she was one of very few women in the hired function room. She was certainly the only one under forty. At first, the attention was flattering, there hadn't been much from the opposite sex in her life. Some of the men she saw attracted her, but it was Gary who had been the first to react. He slid his body along the bar, holding a glass in his hand and cocky grin.

"Here, let me pay for your drink."

"Erm, I already paid for it but thanks."

"Next one's on me, Doll Face," he winked at Jules which made her shudder slightly.

"It's Jules." That had been her first mistake. If only she had stuck with Doll Face.

"Jules…" Gary drew a deep breath of air and focused his gaze on a non-specific spot on the ceiling. Jules thought he looked like a tit and the way he acted like he was inhaling her name made her want to vomit. Unfortunately for Jules the small and uncomfortable chat had been nearly impossible to escape from. She wasn't brave enough to start a conversation with anyone else at the function so endured Gary for most of the evening. By the end he became more insistent about making sure that she got home okay. Jules managed to convince him to let her go it alone in exchange for her phone number, another big mistake. From then on rarely a week went by without at least three or four home visits or phone calls from Gary. The message had been loud and clear on numerous occasions, she wasn't interested in him. But Gary wouldn't take no for an answer. So far, he hadn't proven to be violent and although he was a constant pest, Jules felt sorry for him. At least she did until his recent exile from the local birder club for indecently exposing himself in a nature reserve.

Back in her flat, Jules saw she had a message from a friend asking to meet her and some of the other girls for drinks. She didn't fancy being on her own and girls were good for sharing things with. It would be good to get their views on her Austin dilemma.

They all shared the same opinion as her mum and encouraged her to send the request. Jules' friends teased with good nature about her innocence, all claiming to of done far worse than send a friend request. When she returned home later that night (thankfully no stalkers were awaiting her this time), Jules gained a veil of newfound confidence that was owed to the several glasses of wine – she sent the request. Oh well, it's done now. Despite the alcohol, sleep did not come easy to her that night.

Why oh, why hadn't she set an earlier alarm this morning? Her hair was an unruly mess, everything she tried to do with it just made things worse. Then there was her wardrobe malfunction. The entire contents of which were the malfunction, Jules never gave much thought to her appearance at work up until now. Next Saturday she promised herself, she would get one of the girls to take her shopping. For today she would just have to do her best. She sat nervously behind her desk and tried to keep busy with the usual Monday morning emails, but it was already past nine and Austin was punctual. Before she could check the clock again there was the silhouette of a man walking past her office. It was Austin! She could make him out through the frosted glass that divided her office from the hallway. He seemed to slow his pace for a second before picking it back up again and walking past down the corridor to his own office. There was a sudden sense of relief followed by disappointment. What was she expecting anyway? Was he going to come sweeping into her office pronouncing his undying love for her just because of a stupid friend request? You've got to get a grip girl!

The Flying Contradiction

He shouldn't have been surprised that it was another low budget, no first class, free for all airline. Nor should he be angry that it was the only one with a seat available landing in London, Gatwick – but he was. Bobby had missed Old Blighty, but fucking London? He could never stand the capital despite his love for the Kray twins (one of them at least) from an early age. The place was just too overcrowded and dirty. Everything he'd endured on his previous visits, nothing but disrespect everywhere he'd turned. At least he was on the way back home if only for a short duration. The journey could of course be much improved if it wasn't for his current travelling companions. He'd heard the boy's voice in the departure lounge, as if anyone couldn't! The lad's voice grated upon him immediately fuelling a desire to throttle him there and then. Apparently, the lad would not be content until he had made it crystal clear to the entire Malaga airport that he was gay. That's the way Bobby had seen it – little mincer – he fumed, taking the boy's sexual orientation as a personal slight. He just couldn't understand where they had all come from these days! Bloody parents need to wring it out of them at an early age! He never saw himself as a homophobe, each to their own, but this outward display of one's sexuality gnarled at his patience – he believed campiness should have died out with Carry On films. Bobby had done everything to ensure he was front of the queue, even paying for an early boarding pass. He commended himself for this small privilege when he saw the flamboyant young man join the queue for the same plane. He who dares Bobby, he who dares. The early boarding allowed him to find a window seat with two empty chairs to his left. There had been several agreeable female passengers, but they went on to other seats. A feeling of dread had creeped up his spine when he heard the voice that offended him so much.

"Anyone sitting here luvvy?"

Bobby stared, stunned with momentary disbelief. What the fuck is he wearing?! Bobby took in the tight denim shorts and baggy t-shirt that hung just above the boy's waist. It was the sort of thing he would have had the girls from his club wearing. Not a human man! He was repulsed by this blatant display of disrespect. It's up to you what you do on your time but this… Bobby never got to utter any such words as his fellow passenger, sensing the growing silence took it as a cue to sit down anyway.

"Thank yooou!" the boy said sitting down and gently patting Bobby's knee. "Ooo, you're the silent type. I like those," he giggled. Bobby was too shocked to continue. It wasn't like he'd never seen gay people before. Hell! He even owned a Queen album. But this was just too real for him, he couldn't work out if the boy was being disrespectful or flirting. For once Bobby hoped it was the former as the latter raised too many questions he would rather not deal with. He watched a girl in her late teens wearing too much makeup and against all the odds less clothing than the lad. She stood in the aisle by their row of seats.

"Gemma! Hey babes. Come sit down with us. You don't mind do you luv?" the boy asked.

"No," replied Bobby. Well, at least's he has manners.

"This is Gem Gem, we just met in the airport bar, but we already know we're soul mates don't we Gem Gem?" The girl took her seat.

"Course we are babes!" She turned towards Bobby before adding, "JJ just so like… gets me, you know?"

"Sure. I'm just going to get some sleep, so if you two could… you know," Bobby nestled his head into the wall of the plane and closed his eyes.

"Oh! Poor sleepy head. Ok babes! We'll try!" The pair of them cackled but to Bobby's surprise they actually respected his request and kept conversation to an acceptable level. Just as well he thought. A tin can with over a hundred witnesses wasn't a good place for vengeance.

Bobby didn't know how long he'd been asleep if at all but apparently the keeping quiet hadn't lasted long from his neighbouring passengers. He was awoken by the high-pitched laugh of the boy and the pig like snort from the girl. As his mind readjusted to consciousness he took in their conversation.

"Three days though JJ! I don't think I could go that long without food."

"I just can't risk it Gem Gem. Mr Big always insists on a clean back passage, he even paid to have my arsehole bleached!"

"Oh, you didn't JJ! What was it like?" the girl spluttered inquisitively.

"What? Before I had it done or the having it done?" JJ tittered in amusement. Bobby winced at the image of the boys now bleached bum hole that floated in his mind. An image that was only possible due to the way he ended Diego's life.

"JJ! You're too much!"

"No Gem Gem, Mr Big's too much. He's hung like a bloody mule! I swear last time he went so far up me I could feel him at the back of my tonsils!" Gem Gem and JJ burst into tears of laughter whilst Bobby stifled a gag of rising bile in his throat.

“Can you please keep your sordid tales to yourself young man, not everyone on this plane needs to hear it,” Bobby asked firmly.

“Oh! Hello, Mr sleepy head. Sorrrry. Didn’t know you were awake,” JJ replied.

“Please just keep it down.” The young pair carried on their conversation carefully keeping their voices lower, but Bobby was already too awake with the horrific images in his head and therefore unable to block out the further talk.

“I had to sit on a cushion for a week after the last time.”

“Why do you do it then babes?”

“The money Gem Gem. They all pay me very well, I make sure of that, but Mr Big goes that one step further than the rest. He always wants me at my best. The only thing he scrimps on are the hotels, if you could call them that. I swear he must have a discount card with one chain of budget hotels, that’s where I’m meeting him tonight.”

“Is he picking you up from the airport then?”

“No, he doesn’t go that far, he’ll pay for the taxi though. I’ve got the place to myself until he arrives later tonight then it’s cash up front and all business from behind!” JJ and Gem Gem burst back into fits of barely contained laughter. Bobby couldn't believe what he was hearing, the boy had no decorum. It wasn't as though the act of selling your body for sex was offensive to him, he'd made a good source of his income over the years from the sex trade. That hadn't involved Bobby selling his own skin though and never had he done so through same sex relations.

"He must be loaded then JJ? Who is he? Anyone famous?" the girl asked.

"He's loaded alright but not really famous. He owns a football club. You heard of FFG United?"

"I ain't babes."

"Me neither, but he owns them apparently. Don't be telling anyone though Gem Gem! He's married an all. He'd bloody kill me if it got out."

Oh, I don't think he will. Bobby had heard enough. Everything about the boy had stirred up all sorts of emotional confusion. The directly applied manners he'd shown Bobby would ordinarily be enough to unknowingly save him from unlimited pain. Bobby wondered if the boy had suffered a similar fate to himself, perhaps they had just chosen different paths. The chilling events of Bobby's childhood were deeply buried beneath decades of self-justified violence – dished out to anyone foolish enough to disrespect him. He'd done (in his own eyes) a great job of putting that behind him, at least until he became old enough and strong enough to find the man who his own mother had let into their lives. That had been Bobby's first, his mother had been a close second. Still, it did nothing to stem the confusing urges he'd often felt and until today had kept largely at bay. Something about this Mr Big using the boy churned the feeling back to the forefront of his mind. In the midst of confusion, Bobby decided one thing was for certain. It wouldn't be JJ that Mr Big would be meeting later tonight. The lad wasn't quite off the hook yet though – I have a use for you.

Scrapped

Austin marched, this time, with a rare confidence toward the basement, striding down the corridor up to Jules' office and… he walked right past. As soon as he was in entering distance of the open door, he remembered how useless he was with women. What had he been thinking? Did he really believe that he was just going to walk right in, start some small talk about birds and then what? It just wasn't Austin. He continued down the hall to his own office, reasoning with himself that he had a job to do, which to be fair was absolutely right. There was always later he reassured himself. After all, he couldn't put it off forever, she held the files he needed. For now, he would check his messages. If Phipps hadn't got back to him then at least the scrap yard owner should have replied by now. He checked his answer phone, email and even called the switch board on the off chance that they'd received something but alas, it wasn't to be. Austin found his good mood being severely tested.

It would be unwise to try calling Phipps again. He was harbouring undertones of impatience. And so, he decided to channel his mild temper to the scrap dealer instead.

"Hello, Colney Metals."

"Yes, hello. This is Detective Constable Austin Healey. I called you last week about the Lexus. I was hoping to hear from the owner," Austin replied.

"Oh, yes! The car bloke. My husband said he stripped the Lexus for parts because of the damage."

"Erm, how was the car damaged?"

"A tractor dear. Not much left of the flashy car after the collision apparently."

"Sorry? A tractor hit it?" Austin didn't dare believe his luck – his swagger may yet return in light of such sleuth. Surely an accident of that level would have been reported to the Insurance Company, if not for the highly suspicious Paul Hargreaves, but too for the driver of the agricultural vehicle. It wasn't uncommon for drivers to settle the damage without involving Insurance Companies, nor was it illegal but not the usual behaviour of a police sergeant. He needed to push for more information, "Was the tractor also scrapped?"

"No dear, I think it escaped without a scratch."

"Do you know who the tractor belonged to then, Mrs McKay?"

"Oh, yes of course dear."

“And could you tell me the driver’s name?” Austin couldn’t tell if she was being intentionally evasive or whether the lady was just a few sandwiches short of a picnic. He took a breath and continued the parley.

“And could you give me that name please Mrs McKay?”

“Oh, yes. Mr McKay.”

Obviously, this wasn’t going anywhere fast he groaned, “No, not your husband’s name. The tractor driver’s name.”

“Yes dear. It was Mr McKay.”

“Your husband was driving the tractor?” He wondered if there was a bad line her end.

“Oh, no dear. That’s Don’s tractor you see.”

“So why was Mr McKay, your husband, driving it?”

“My husband wasn’t driving the tractor dear.”

Darren Somerville, blowing it with Jules, and the senior officer’s dog shit jibes rushed to the forefront of Austin’s mind – he snapped, “WHO WAS DRIVING THE BLOODY TRACTOR THEN?!”

“Well there’s no need to get shirty dear,” Mrs McKay said with hurt in her voice.

"Sorry... Mrs McKay, who was driving the tractor on the day that it collided with the Lexus belonging to Sergeant Paul Hargreaves?"

"Don McKay."

Austin stared at the phone in disbelief before the conversation finally eased and slotted into Austin's logic.

"Jon's my husband, Don's his brother."

Clearly the McKay's parents hadn't been as inventive as his own when it came to name giving. But, finally, Austin was getting somewhere.

"Do you have a contact number for Don McKay, Madam?"

"Oh, I don't know if I could just give out that sort of information dear."

"Madam, may I remind you I am an officer of the law. I am inspecting an open criminal case and withholding information is a criminal offence."

"Well I don't know about all that dear. There's no need for threats and anyway, DCI Chilcot dealt with the incident. I'm afraid I can't tell you any more than that, if you need anything else, you'll have to contact your colleagues in the local police force," and with that Mrs McKay hung up the phone.

DCI Chilcot – Austin, pen in hand, he knew the name. He was up there with the very best of them, a true legend of the force and if Austin's memory served him correctly then Chilcot was Phipps' former superior. But hadn't Chilcot retired years ago? Nothing was adding up.

Austin would contact Phipps again, after he of course had checked Chilcot's file. He needed to know that the man had retired before wading in too strong. There was also the matter of the 'local police force', Austin was surprised that a town small as Colney would have anything that could be called a 'force'. At the most there would be a sergeant, constable and at a push a PCO, anyone more superior would have been drafted in from the governing constabulary.

A brief internet search confirmed to Austin that he was indeed right. Colney had a local safer neighbourhood team consisting of Sergeant Fred Hirst and PC Martin Spettigue. There was certainly no current officer with the rank of Detective Chief Inspector. A crime as innocuous as a fender bender wasn't befitting of a police officer with such authority. Austin could believe a police sergeant such as Hargreaves may have been transferred to Colney but why then was there no record of it? He accessed the police records online to check a DCI Chilcot, but that had showed retirement almost ten years ago when the highly decorated officer held the rank of Chief Superintendent. On top of that, Chilcot had never worked in Colney.

His last role had been in Avon and Somerset, an entirely different jurisdiction to the area governed by Devon and Cornwall police. Any further digging on the man would need clearance from Austin's superior, something he would certainly be seeking from Bragg. But, before he could do that, he would need to pick up the case file and that meant seeing Jules. Well, he'd put it off enough already… on second thoughts, maybe he would try calling Phipps' department again.

Braggart

Chief Superintendent Bragg pulled his car over as soon as he saw "the name" calling his mobile. Ordinarily he would have ignored the call until he arrived at the station but when the Chief Inspector of Avon and Somerset called, you answered. "Chief Inspector. What a pleasant surprise, how can I help?" Bragg didn't notice that his voice had risen a couple of octaves.

"Cut all that shit out Bragg. I've got a bone to pick with you. Who the bloody hell is this Austin Healey and why is he digging into the history of my officers?"

Bragg spluttered in surprise, trying to choke out a response.

"Stop babbling like a pleb and answer me Bragg. Why didn't you contact me first? He's one of yours', isn't he?"

"Yes, erm, sorry Sir. Yes, Austin is, but I'm afraid I don't know what you're referring too. He's been reassigned to cold cases, nothing interesting in them I promise you. I ran through them myself, none of them indicated any other police officers' wrongdoings."

"Well he's stumbled across something Bragg. Something I don't need some low ranked bastard sticking his nose into. Leaving enquiries with my branch for anyone to get hold of, what the hell are you running over there?"

"Chief Inspector I can assure you, that this must be a mistake. Healey's an honest cop, a little too honest sometimes. There must be some mistake. Who has he been asking after?"

"Never you mind Bragg. Don't you realise we have undercover officers in the field? I can't have this jumped up little shit putting them at risk, can I?" Phipps lied. At least it was a half-truth. "If you can't keep an eye on your staff maybe we need to find someone else who can."

"No! I mean, no Sir. I will, I mean I can, I already do. Oh, that little bastard will be spoken to, don't you worry about that Sir. I'll drag him into my office as soon as I get to the station. He's on thin ice as it is, yes. Yes, some discipline is in order," Bragg snivelled.

"Just tell him to back off Bragg or you and I will be having further words."

The line went dead as Bragg stared at the blank screen with trembling hands. That Fucking Healey! He would be dealing with him alright. Last warning this time or Austin was going to find himself handing out speeding tickets. Like most of the entire Yeovil police department, Bragg couldn't stand Healey. He inherited the detective constable when he'd taken over as chief superintendent. Austin was a jobsworth but due to his superior detective skills served his purpose numerous times. Healey would have been promoted at least once by now if he didn't have the habit of stepping on his colleague's toes. The man just couldn't learn to let some things slide.

Bragg was only five minutes away from the station but the embarrassment he'd just endured at the hands of Phipps made him act instinctively. He unlocked the phone in his still shaking hands and called Austin Healey.

"Good morning sir, I'm glad you called. I was hoping to speak to you ab…" Austin never got to finish.

"Speak to me! Oh, we'll be fucking speaking alright Healey! Get your interfering poncey arse up to my fucking office right fucking now! Wait for me outside." Bragg won some of his self-respect back by slamming the phone down on Austin. Yes, shit ran downhill!

Almost

Austin could feel the sweat trickling down from his armpits on the

walk towards Jules' office. Fortunately, it was cold in the basement so the damp patches appearing on his shirt were covered by the justified suit jacket. This was it! This time he would talk to Jules properly. No more awkward conversation. No more babbling about case files. The call he made to Phipps' office was picked up by the same lady he'd spoken to the other day and he surprised himself at making small talk with a member of the opposite sex. Austin had against all odds even made a joke at his own expense which made the woman laugh. It was all the practice he needed. Now for the real thing and here he was, a mere foot away from Jules office door. He would have gone in too. No, really, he would. Except as he inched towards the door his phone rang. He stopped and took a few paces back away from the open door and looked at the caller ID. Bragg. Oh, good! Just the man I need to talk to. Austin answered his phone.

"Good morning sir, I'm glad you called. I was hoping to speak to you ab…"

XXX

He didn't have to wait long before Bragg came storming down the corridor, flaring his nose like a bull ready to charge down a matador.

"Get in there Healey!"

Austin had obliged like a scolded child, sheepishly leading the way into his superior officer's private room. Bragg slammed the door shut making the window blinds fly up and whack the door several times. Austin went to sit at one of the chairs in front of the desk that Bragg sat behind.

"Did I tell you to sit Healey? No! You don't get to fucking sit. You stupid, interfering little shit… Why are you a constant bane of my life? Why can't you learn to play the fucking game Healey? No one likes you here, it's getting harder to justify your being here at all."

Austin stood stunned in silence. What had he done now? He'd hoped the incident with the influential dogger might have died down by now. He didn't care about the insults being hurled at him, but he would never swallow any attack to his moral status.

"Why have you been going over my head calling Chief Inspector Phipps? You trying to get me in the shit, you little… shit?"

Austin was so confused his head spun. Why had Phipps called Bragg about his innocent inquiry? If the chief inspector had received his message, then why not contact Austin himself? Sergeant Paul Hargreaves' name had obviously hit a nerve. What was it about this man?

"Guv, I am truly sorry. I meant no disrespect to you at all. I was just following up a lead on the cold cases. You see this Sergeant Paul..."

"Shut up Healy! I don't want to hear another word about it. What? Did you think you'd give Phipps a little call and get all pally? Think you could get yourself a little transfer or move up the ladder, did you?"

"N, no sir!"

"N, n, n, shut the fuck up!" Bragg mimicked Austin's nervous stammer, flecks of spittle flying over the desktop.

"Drop the case Healey, move on. And don't you ever go over my fucking head like that again. You come to me if you find anything. If I hear you've called Phipps or any other senior officer before speaking to me first, you're suspended. Okay Constable?"

Mmm? Had Phipps called Bragg before or after he had left the message about Chilcot?

"I said okay Constable?"

"Eh, yes Guv. Sorry Guv…" Austin trailed off wondering whether it would be best to mention Chilcot now or just leave it. Sod it! He didn't think it was possible to make things any worse at this point. Bragg shook his head at the pondering constable.

"What is it Healey? Spit it out then get out."

"Guv, have you heard of DCI Chilcot?"

Bragg shook his head in astonishment. "Get out Healey. Now! And don't let the door knock out your teeth on the way!"

As he made his way back down to the basement, Austin waved goodbye to his good mood. He knew it couldn't last; nothing ever did in his experience. He would be walking a very fine line from now on, that had been made crystal clear by Bragg. And for what? Doing his job. Austin knew that the detective in him couldn't let it go. The mystery of Hargreaves was too intriguing so perhaps his earlier suspicion of the missing sergeant being undercover was true. But Chilcot? A retired officer in his late sixties was hardly undercover material. There was something going on here and Austin would find out one way or the other. Finally, he was beginning to think that playing by the rules wasn't working for him. He'd have to be careful: it would do no good to his future development if he was demoted. It was time for a change – no more Mr 'Nice' Healey. He was so caught up in thought he hadn't realised that he was walking right past Jules' office.

Austin back tracked and walked directly into the room, she looked up as he stood in front of her, this time he forced himself to maintain eye contact. Jules caught off guard with a half-eaten Pepperami hanging from one side of her mouth, Austin had nothing to lose.

"Guv?" Jules managed to force the single syllable out around the processed meat.

"Morning Jules. Erm, I've been meaning to ask… I mean, what I'm trying to say is…" Here goes nothing. "Jules, are you free tonight? I'd rather like to take you out for dinner."

He did it! He actually bloody did it! Austin was changing for the better. This time nothing could spoil his mood, not even the half-chewed stick off meat that dropped out of Jules' now vacant mouth.

Let the Games Begin

Sipping the last of the complimentary coffee, Bobby relaxed on top of the hotel bed sheets. He'd wrapped himself in the dressing gown provided and waited in comfort. It hadn't been easy getting JJ to part with the room, but then Bobby Cavendish was very persuasive. The boy's face when he knocked on the door had been one of surprise and much to Bobby's distaste, lustful. JJ hadn't wanted to open up about his early years at first, especially to Bobby, who treated homosexuality as an illness. Bobby had played the concerned councillor, but it didn't give him the incite he was hoping for. The boy just couldn't see the good Bobby was trying to do, even trying to escape the room. Perhaps there was confusion as to why a stranger from a plane had taken a sudden interest in his upbringing. It would have seemed peculiar to anyone – except Bobby Cavendish. In the end he'd had to 'let him go' after he gleamed all possible information of Mr Big. It was a terrible shame. Bobby had grown quite fond of JJ.

In the somewhat speculative minutes before Mr Big arrived, Bobby took advantage of the paid-for room and all its amenities. After a well needed shower, he waited for his guest. At nine PM the door handle turned and in walked the bloated balding man, sixties, already with a bulging erection that was visible through his trousers. The lecherous look on Mr

Big's face contorted to disgust when he saw Bobby sitting cross legged in his hotel room chair.

"Who the fuck are you? You're not the boy! You don't even look anywhere near young enough!" Face reddening as the blood from his erection pumped to his upper body, Mr Big's jowls glowed, excited none-the-less, his toad-pulsing neck gloating, contradicting, feeding his own expectations. "He better not have fucked off with my money and sent you instead. No… No! I'm not having it. Where is JJ?"

"Come sit down," Bobby stood up in his new hotel dressing gown and patted the bed. "JJ will be along soon. I'm just going to… get you set up." Bobby was proud of his acting skills – it had taken him a lot of discipline to play the part. The man grumbled and reluctantly did as he was bid, awkwardly undressing his entitlements.

"No! Wait… keep them on for just a bit longer. All in good time." There was a limit to Bobby's method acting and seeing the grotesque man's body was just that. It was Mr Big's response that had escalated the scene to the next stage, Bobby was only too relieved.

"Don't you tell me what to do! Little cunt. What are you anyway? Sixty?"

Sixty? The disrespect! Bobby momentarily forgot that he wasn't actually a rent boy. And as if the mental image of this rancid old man defiling his sweet friend hadn't been enough already – dear JJ.

Let the games begin!

XXX

It had been a good one. One of his best. It had turned out that cheap hotel rooms held a treasure trove of useful items needed for one's torturous needs. Coat hangers, kettles, light fixtures, TV remotes, disposable toothbrushes and even a Gideon's bible had all come in handy. It was the spoon from the tea and coffee set that brought everything to a stop. Maybe it did end the fun prematurely, but Bobby became wary of the sickening sound of death Mr Big was emitting 'towards' the end – the cleaning staff would be busy for weeks Bobby chuckled. Unbeknown however to Bobby, the hotel staff and guests put the braying sounds down to an unusual sex game. Something not so uncommon for patrons visiting the budget hotels. Two in one day! Sleep came naturally for Bobby.

At sunrise, Bobby collected what he needed from the freshly deceased and bloated Mr Big – wallet, JJ's escort card, license, house keys and a Jaguar key chain. Before leaving, Bobby paid for another two nights using the deceased's credit card. For extra measure he left the 'do not disturb' sign on the handle. Cameras in the hotel didn't worry him, he wouldn't be in the country long enough and, well, by this point he couldn't even give a shit if Phipps or Chilcot knew about it. They could clean up the mess that the cleaners missed.

Finding Mr Big's car had been easy enough, clicking the Jaguar's key fob until the sportscar flashed back at him. If he had to drive himself, then he might as well do it with style.

And so, Bobby, his thirst for violence quenched, hit the road playing Killer Queen at full volume, hoping he could make the trip in one go and avoid another public encounter. He really shouldn't have had that last coffee – Bobby had always suffered from a weak bladder.

A Mouthful of Meat

Jules was in the process of correcting everybody's reports when Austin's phone began to ring just outside her office. Whatever the call was about, it must have been urgent, for Austin engaged a quickened pace straight past. He was a good police officer by her reckoning. He'd been called off to something more important upstairs. Perhaps she wouldn't see him again today. Stupid, so stupid. Why did she send that drunken request? It had just made things more awkward for them both. After finishing her current workload, she decided to treat herself to a Peperami. Jules chanced that Austin wouldn't be coming down again any time soon. She didn't think the image of her chewing on a meaty protein stick would have been altogether flattering – she didn't know how wrong she was. Her fingers carried on typing, leaving her mouth to do the work on the salami snack. Jules sensed static in the air, felt the butterflies in her stomach before the sound of footsteps, someone standing in the doorway before she had time to react. It was Austin, staring intently at her.

"Guv?" Jules managed to force the single syllable out around the processed meat.

“Morning Jules. Erm, I’ve been meaning to ask… I mean, what I’m trying to say is…Jules, are you free tonight? I’d really like to take you to dinner.”

The sausage tumbled from her lips onto the desk. The two second delay felt like an eternity as Jules’ brain scrambled the single syllable response to her vocal cords.

“Yes!”

Sexy Sausage

Austin's heart froze in upon itself within the time he waited for Jules to reply. And what seemed to last a lifetime allowed him to regret his sudden confidence – the 'give a fuck' approach spawned from his rock bottom meeting with Bragg. The time he took to doubt himself and question why a woman who could look stunning even with a half-eaten meat stick hanging from her mouth. Then the unthinkable happened and it was his turn to take too long to respond.

"…erm… great! …So, shall I pick you up or meet you there? Sorry I'm not very good at this."

"Where do you want to go Guv?" Jules winced as she used the formal title instead of Austin.

"Well, there's a really nice Indian I know and please, call me Austin."

"Sounds great to me… Austin. I can meet you anywhere, just give me a time and the name of the place… thank you."

"I'll send you the details on Facepage. Thanks for the request, by the way. I meant to tell you this morning."

"Thank you for accepting! I was beginning to feel really stupid…"

"No, please don't, sorry Jules. I was going to come and see you I really was, but I got called upstairs by the chief."

"Yeah, I saw you go, is everything okay?"

Everything was most certainly okay. Well, maybe not with his boss but that didn't seem to matter right now. Austin was feeling like a new man. This date proposal was so much easier than he'd ever imagined.

"Yes, yes I think everything is going to be really okay now. Well, Chief Superintendent Bragg isn't very pleased, but I er…" Austin realised he was babbling, he just needed to say his bit and quit while he was ahead. "Never mind, I'll explain later. See you later Jules."

"I can't wait."

Austin hesitated not knowing what to do with himself before deciding to shake Jules hand and leave the room. It wasn't smooth but she didn't mind. They were going on a date!

Opening Old Wounds

If Phipps had been angry after his phone call with Bragg, then it was safe to say he was now incandescent with rage. It was all he could do to contain his professional manner when the receptionist had passed on the second message from Austin Healey. Digging into Hargreaves was one thing but mentioning Chilcot's name had pushed him too far. This Austin must have found something on Hargreaves if he was bringing Chilcot into it too. If Bragg couldn't deal with his officers properly then he would have to take matters into his own hands and that wouldn't benefit either of the inferior ranked men. When he and Chilcot had dealt with Hargreaves and Cavendish, everything had been watertight – so he thought.

Four years earlier – Colney village

Phipps found the Ivy Tavern, the heart of that little village. He admired the rural look of the building with its spreading vines engulfing the pub. The summer had ended early giving way to torrential downpours and an overcast sky. Today however, the sun made a rare appearance adding to its picturesque setting. A good omen? Phipps could only hope entering the bustling pub. He spotted his former mentor and father figure propping up the bar with a collection of locals all vying for his attention. Chilcot beamed at the sight of Phipps, raising his glass in greeting.

"Alan. You made it," Chilcot turned back to the bar, "Harry, get this man a drink."

Phipps walked up to the popular man who threw both arms around him, "So good to see you Charlie! What's it been? A year already?"

"Alan you shouldn't be a stranger dear boy. You know you're always welcome here. After all, you already contributed dearly to the village festival," Chilcot chuckled at their private joke and released Phipps.

"I know Charlie, but these criminals won't arrest themselves, so run off our feet these days. We could do with having you back on the force."

Chilcot roared with laughter setting off a handful of the nearby punters, so infectious was the big man's joviality. "Those days are well and truly behind me lad. These fine people are my flock now and I am sworn as their shepherd. Though, it pains me to admit that I'm not sure that I can live up to the honour they have afforded me for much longer."

Phipps tried to object but Chilcot silenced him with a dismissive hand. "Come, sit down with me Alan. We have a lot to discuss."

The two of them walked over to a quiet corner seat. Chilcot gestured for Phipps to sit before taking a chair opposite.

"So, have you been behaving Phippsy? Hmm?"

Phipps chortled with embarrassment. He knew what the man meant. Chilcot had covered for Phipps in the past with his mild abuse of the law. After the help he'd given Chilcot and his wife locating their niece's killer – Paul Hargreaves – and getting Bobby Cavendish off the streets, he'd eyed redemption. Admittedly he had come clean about his involvement with Cavendish. The extra earnings in exchange for looking the other way so that Bobby could continue his criminal empire. Phipps found it highly contradictive of his former boss, who forged a new career here in this village, sacrificing criminals rather than turning them over to the justice system. Not that Phipps disagreed with Colney's rituals – each to their own. Instead he simply replied, "Of course Charlie! Ha. I mean, we got them in the end, didn't we? Both are gone now and can't cause any more harm."

"Is that so? Well, that's true for one of them at least. Bobby Cavendish on the other hand is walking free without punishment. In fact, he did rather well out of this deal. Perhaps better than all of us…" Chilcot took a sip of his beer deep in thought.

Phipps wasn't sure what to do with the awkward silence. "Cavendish claimed he was in love with Hannah, or Emily as he knew her."

He waited for Chilcot to speak but was met with more silence. "All his illegal enterprises were shut down and he had to forego his name… we did the right thing Charlie."

Chilcot crashed down his fist like a judge's gavel making Phipps regret his words. "Did we Alan? Did we really? Yes, we dealt with that bastard who killed her… my niece!" The meaty hand came down softer this time. "He was one of yours! Rotten to the core, an insult to the force. How didn't you know Alan?"

Alan Phipps did have an inkling. After all, it was he who assigned Hargreaves to the case. The former undercover officer had been the ideal candidate. Paul Hargreaves had worked his way under Phipps' skin from the off. The man was an arrogant bigot. Someone like him was bound to blow his cover long before he got anywhere near Cavendish. Phipps had pushed Hargreaves ahead of other much more competent officers. Those who might stumble upon Phipps' back handers from Cavendish, even going so far as to remove another officer from the role. One who had come too close – Quinlan. But to his surprise, Hargreaves' contact had informed Phipps about the man's rise in the Cavendish empire. Maybe he wasn't as incompetent as first believed. After that Phipps kept a close interest in the undercover operation, already working out how this might profit him – Phipps did very much like the money.

“I’m sorry Charlie. I’ve told you before, he was a rotten apple. Nobody expected what he was capable of, not even Cavendish.”

Chilcot managed to calm himself down but his body looked like the fit of anger had taken the wind out of him. Phipps could see how much the man had aged. “I know Alan. I know. It’s still raw to me, that’s all,” Chilcot’s charming smile returned. “Now, Alan. I didn’t invite you all the way out here just for the social visit. Not entirely. I have some news, both good and bad.”

Phipps straightened himself in the chair, “I’m all ears Charlie.”

“Quite. I’m dying Alan… cancer. It’s not treatable and believe me I’ve heard it all before so don’t bother...” Phipps tried to interject to offer his apologies but Chilcot shut him down, “… Alice bless her, keeps telling me to find a second opinion or search for experimental treatment, but I won’t have it. I know! I can feel its grip on me Alan. The buggers winning this battle.”

“Charlie, I’m so sorry to hear. Are you sure there isn’t anything they can do?” Phipps was shaken by the news. Although they hadn’t spent as much time together these days, Chilcot was his friend, his mentor and so much more. There would be dark times ahead.

"Now, come on Alan. I've already told you not to do that. It is what it is, let us speak no more of it."

"Christ's sake Charlie! At least tell me how long you've got?" Phipps couldn't believe how blasé the man was being about it.

"Anything from six months to a year, maybe a bit more if I do their medication. Now, seriously. I want to talk to you about something else, the good news." Phipps hoped it was very good news after the bad.

"Once I'm gone, the village will need a new protector. It's tradition for the locals to choose somebody but I would very much like to put you forward to the committee…"

Phipps' head swam. It was a lot to take in for one day.

"… it's a happy life here Alan. They pay incredibly well, and I know you have your eye on the position."

It was true, Phipps had been in awe of the respect and salary Chilcot received from running the small parish. The whole place had a magnetism which drew him in.

"I'm sure you're not thinking about leaving the force yet, but in the future. I'll understand if you're not ready. There are others who can hold fort if I pass before that time."

Phipps was unquestionably ready. He'd been ready two days into his current role. All he did now was interviews and paperwork. Long gone was the real policework, the sort of stuff that allowed you to dip your fingers into the pie. But this job, this would do him nicely. The wage – the popularity – and what about the nearby golf courses! Sacrificing the odd criminal on a burning stake… Sometimes you have to get your hands dirty.

"This is a lot to think about Charlie… I mean with your illness…"

"Cancer, Alan," Chilcot reminded.

"Yes… with the sad news and now this too," Phipps really hoped he was playing it cool enough.

"Don't try beating round the bush with me. Do you want the job Alan?" Chilcot asked flatly.

"Erm, well. Yes, yes I would be honoured Charlie."

"Okay. But it comes on one condition…"

Phipps gulped. He didn't like the sound of that.

"You've got to find Bobby Cavendish…"

That was easy enough, Phipps knew the exact address.

"… and kill him."

That might prove trickier. Bobby Cavendish was an animal who delighted in murder – Phipps was… Phipps. He'd cross that bridge later – he really wanted the job.

"I'll do it."

XXX

A week passed as Phipps played out scenarios where he took Cavendish's life. No matter how much he tried to fool himself, he knew that it was fantasy. It wasn't for the guilt of taking the ex-gangster's existence – Phipps couldn't care one way or the other – it was the fear of failing. The very idea of his own cessation terrified him, even more so at the hands of the notorious man who excelled in prolonged death. So, by the time he landed in Malaga airport, Phipps decided on a different strategy. One that would suit all parties. Simply asking a man like Bobby Cavendish to pretend he was dead was far too risky. The man was a self-righteous, egotistical maniac. There was no way someone of Bobby Cavendish's ilk would stay away forever, even if it did mean arrest. The money they'd paid – a deposit in credit – wouldn't last forever, Phipps knew that. What he needed was a financial incentive to keep Bobby away – and the problem – Phipps was broke. He'd been out of the game too long to know who ran the criminal underworld anymore, much less extort their cash. Phipps suspected there was another way. Cavendish couldn't have risen to his position if he didn't have knowledge of someone or somewhere where he could find some. It was perilous, not just because of Cavendish's unpredictable behaviour but if Chilcot found out that Phipps denied him his dying wish – the job would be the last of his worries.

The drive to the villa had been a pig of a journey. Several times Phipps had lost his way and was thankful to find a small settlement that he likened to a shanty town nearby. The locals had pointed him in the right direction after putting his limited Spanish to the test. The smoke rising into the sky from the distance acted as a beacon, guiding Phipps to the brilliant white isolated villa. The smell was sickening, like charred meat gone bad in the Mediterranean heat. As Phipps stopped the rental vehicle outside the gates, he wondered how Bobby Cavendish would take to his unplanned visit. It wasn't as if they traded phone numbers after Bobby's exile. Much to his surprise the gnawing sick feeling in the pit of his stomach had been unwarranted. Cavendish in fact had been ecstatic for the surprise company ushering Phipps into the property and past the suspicious fire.

"Police officer Phipps! Ha. What do I owe this pleasure? What, no Chilcot? Shame, we could have had some fun together."

Bobby poured out two glasses of red wine. A legendary vintage he bragged. Phipps wasted no time – he didn't want to extend his visit any more than was necessary. As he relayed Chilcot's request, omitting the man's illness, Bobby sat patiently. Not once did he show anger, rather, bemused interest.

"So, keeping me from my one true love's funeral wasn't enough for the greedy fucker? Now he's sent his minion to do his dirty work hey. I could have killed his wife you know. It was with respect that I let her live."

"Mr Cavendish…"

"Call me Bobby, or should I say Hargreaves. Oops…"

"Yes, Bobby. I know you gave up a lot to come here. I respect that which is why I come to you with a different solution."

"Oh, I'm all ears Mr Phipps. Do tell…"

"I don't wish to kill you Mr Cav… Bobby…"

Bobby imitated a fearful face which set Phipps instantly on edge. "… not that I believe I could of course. I don't doubt your many talents. I need you to stay dead, Chilcot can't know you're alive. Ever."

"What's in this for me Mr Phipps? Shouldn't I just head back to Blighty now and kill that bloated hog myself? Why, only recently I toyed at the idea of visiting my darling Emily's grave…" Bobby feigned a moment of grief, at least that's what it looked like to Phipps. Little did he know that this was the closest display of real affection Bobby was capable of. "… I could make a trip of it. Maybe visit some of my old haunts and pick up some funds along the way."

Let the dog see the rabbit!

"Bobby, that is exactly what I wanted to talk to you about. I'm sure you know the risk you would be taking returning back to England. The authorities may think you're dead but do all of your previous associates? We made a deal, if you break that then what is to keep me from doing the same?" Phipps knew he was pushing his luck, but he hadn't come unprepared.

"Break the fucking deal?! Then what the fuck is Chilcot doing? You dare to come to my house and threaten me Mr Phipps? If you know me as well as you think then surely you realise that your life is in my hands right now?"

It was time for Phipps to play his wild card, "Mr Cavendish. I may not be a murderer, but may I remind you that I hold the most senior rank possible. I did not come to this elevated position without at least having some smarts. That is why I have left two sealed envelopes with your real name and location with my solicitors. If I do not return by the end of the week then that information shall be passed onto the British media and my employer. They read the red tops in jail you know. Not all of the criminals you sacrificed from your empire are serving long sentences." He hoped the bluff was enough. Bobby stared daggers at him, the silence toxic. Had he gone too far? Phipps was about to try and backtrack when Bobby burst into hysterics.

"You slippery fucker Phipps! Well played, well played indeed. If only the poor bastard on the barbecue outside had your smarts."

The realisation of the smouldering pile's contents shook fear into Phipps. He knew that Bobby had meant it as a threat.

"Okay, Mr Phipps. Enlighten me."

"We can help each other Mr Cavendish. I can locate your money, minus a small fee and in return you promise to stay out of England forever. Not only that but you must have no contact with Chilcot or any of his family. He can not know you are alive." Phipps really hoped the 'fee' wasn't overstepping the mark, but he had to make it worth his while. House prices in Colney weren't cheap.

Bobby clapped his hands, "You know what Phipps? I like you. You're a brazen son-of-a-bitch, I'll give you that… a small fee…" Bobby clapped again. "Why shouldn't I just tell you to fuck off and get the money myself?"

Phipps dug deep for a shred of confidence, "Because if you do, I'll be waiting. I'll tell Chilcot I couldn't do it and I'll let one of your old friends know that you're coming."

Bobby sipped from his wine glass, savouring the claret and pondering the threat.

"Okay. We have a deal. I'll tell you where the money is Phipps but it's down to you to work out how you get it to me. I'm sure with the help of the law you can launder it somehow. I trust you still have Paul Hargreaves' bank details. Ten percent, that's your cut. No more."

Phipps considered negotiating for more but sensed he'd ridden his luck for the day. "We have a deal Mr Cavendish," Phipps stood up and extended his hand, now eager to put as much distance between himself and the psychopath as he could. Bobby stood up and shook the hand, "Bobby, please. We're friends now, Alan."

Bobby wrote down the information Alan Phipps would need. They walked to the door and past the burning human remains; Bobby whispered into Phipps' ear "Don't let that be you Mr Phipps."

XXX

After returning home to the safety of England, Phipps carried out the plan. The guilt of lying to Chilcot was almost as bad as the fear he'd endured in Bobby Cavendish's company – almost. If Cavendish kept his end of the bargain, all he had to do was cover his own tracks. Nobody, no-one was going to find out about Bobby.

Somerset, England – Present day

Who the hell did this Healey think he was? Everything that Phipps had built his career on in the last five years – hanging in the balance of this interfering fuckwit. Phipps had to admit blame for missing the damning evidence left in the cold case, but Healey had to be made to leave it alone! The way he handled his upcoming punishment was pivotal to the detective's livelihood. Chilcot had always been on the lookout for new additions to his precious town's tradition. In all truth, Phipps had always found the whole scarecrow thing a tad strange, but he also had a great respect for Chilcot and every intention of helping to continue the man's legacy. He didn't think it was time for such drastic measures just yet and in any rate, being the clean and honest policeman didn't fit the profile. Chilcot probably wouldn't have approved, but at least it was a backup option. For now, he would try a more peaceful solution and give Bragg a final chance to save his own neck. Phipps made the call.

"Chief Inspector? Twice in one day, what an honour. I can assure you I have dealt with our little problem."

"Our problem Bragg? Listen to me you slimy little bastard, this is your problem and yours alone. It is not my position on the force that's in question here. Healey's called my office again and this time he's really pushing the wrong buttons. Now I'm going to offer you a small bit of decency but that's all you're getting."

"But sir! I did talk to him, I really did. Straight after I spoke to you. I truly gave it to him, Chief Inspector."

Phipps recalled that the lady at his reception said she'd called him straight away. It was possible the call had come before he'd spoken with Bragg. Giving benefit of the doubt, Phipps would offer Bragg one more chance to set things straight.

"I'm going to extend you this one kindness Bragg. It's possible that he made the second call before I spoke to you. I'll give you that much at least but I want this done properly this time. I want him suspended."

"But Chief Inspector, Healey's just too clean! What reason can I give to suspend him? I've already demoted him to cold cases because of him trying to arrest a highly influential member of the Masonic brotherhood. What if he takes it up with the union?"

"I don't know Bragg – fucking hell, must I do everything for you? How the bloody hell did you ever make rank? Think outside of the box, there's always something you can get them on. I don't give a flying fuck if he appeals just get rid of him for a few weeks so I can sort things out my end."

"I'll do my best I promise sir."

"Do better than that, Bragg, or it'll be you next. Do I make myself clear Chief Superintendent?"

Phipps didn't wait for Bragg's response; he couldn't stand the sound of the weaselly man a minute longer.

He'd never known Bragg, but what little he did was enough that he'd do anything to save his own skin. Phipps just hoped the man was capable of sorting out the mess that now threatened his own retirement plans. Nobody was going to fuck that up for him, he was determined to stick to the plan he and Chilcot had set up these years before. Even if he himself had made slight alterations behind his mentor's back. What Chilcot didn't know hadn't hurt him, besides the trip to Spain had benefitted both Bobby and him – a police pension only went so far! Phipps was done with all the political bollocks that came with his job title. His reward was past due.

The Cock and The Hen

Finding the right outfit had been surprisingly difficult for Austin.

You wouldn't think it that hard seeing as his entire ensemble of clothing consisted of nearly the exact same suit. He admitted defeat to the newest one in his possession. Jules wouldn't notice it was the same colour grey as that he wore earlier that day. He made a mental note to take himself shopping at the weekend, if there was a second date. A big if in Austin's mind – he didn't fancy his chances. But against all odds she had said yes, something as unlikely as seeing a Golden Oriole. Jules was a rare bird indeed. No member of the opposite sex had said yes to going out on a date with him before (not that he'd asked). Contrary to Austin's frigid character he had at least lost his virginity; a far from pleasant experience. Tina, she'd made all the moves. Austin had just enrolled into the police program at the time and perhaps owing to his then friendship with Darren Somerville caught her eye. The fact that she was off her head on Sambuca was lost on Austin, but then it had also been one of the rare times he himself was intoxicated. A truly awful experience of cack-handed-fumbling and premature ejaculation. Tina didn't hide her disappointment to Austin or any of their social group. The shameful experience had shown Austin what he wasn't looking for in a woman. He'd decided right there and then he was done with women for good. That was until Jules.

As promised, they exchanged messages via the social media platform and arranged a time. They each decided to find their own way there as Jules had some errands to run in town. Privately, Austin had been relieved, he wanted to get to the table early giving him a chance to swallow some Dutch courage in the form of a light lager – it would be enough for his low alcohol tolerance. He made small talk with the staff, all of whom were familiar to Austin as he was a regular patron. The owner had been overjoyed when Austin had made the booking for two. They weren't used to diners eating out on their own as was usually Austin's custom. Manik Miah, had grown accustomed to Austin's solo visits to his establishment and had a fondness for the police officer. When he realised Austin was on a date, he offered to pull out all the stops for the evening. Austin politely refused, fearing any special attention would embarrass him and Jules. A good decision as Jules would have recoiled in horror under the spotlight. Mr Miah was obviously disappointed that he couldn't help his favourite customer. By way of appeasement, Austin accepted the owner's offer of an extra poppadum for each of them. An excited Mr Miah led Austin to the table himself having not quite given up and pushed the idea of a single red rose to be laid on the table. Austin refused again and instead ordered a lager. Slowly nursing the hoppy liquid from the bottle teat, he tried his best to stop playing out the different scenarios in his mind about the evening ahead. He still had a big decision to make, to pursue this Hargreaves business or do as he'd been told and drop it. It wasn't in his nature to drop a case, and neither was going against orders. What conflicted Austin the most was the rancid odour of corruption that surrounded the investigation, why would Phipps want him away from it so badly and why the secrecy shrouding Chilcot. His attention stolen – the most beautiful sight came walking through the restaurant doors. Jules stood elegantly in the entrance, a look on her face of childlike innocence as she waited for one of the waiters to see to her. Austin eyed a minor disagreement between the staff over who should be the one to attend to their favourite customer's date. Mr Miah seemingly won the staff battle and walked over in greeting. Austin groaned at the display of over accentuated manners as the manager led Jules towards the table. Austin gasped at the knee length dress she was wearing – flattering every inch of her in a way that made him fear standing. To complete the perfect vision, the dress was patterned with pictures of owls. What style! He would definitely have to go on that shopping trip.

On the Road Again

The Jag handled beautifully – it really was a smooth drive. Bobby

had no love for Jaguar's before – he was a Mercedes man. If Mr Big had owned a BMW or AUDI it would have made life hard for Bobby when locating it in the car park – they were ten to a dozen these days. No. The Jag was nice. Aside from the heartache of being in a different country to his beloved Estela, Bobby was feeling pretty good. Both Mr Big and JJ had been carrying a healthy amount of cocaine between them. Along with the coke, Bobby had found some vague looking pills – he saved them for later – the coke now depleted. He hadn't always been this way, unlike the typical stereotype of Montana gangster's, Bobby was different. He'd always had his handle on the drugs when he was running Bristol's underworld. The troubles started when he stopped selling and started buying… that was it! His life was missing not just Estela's love, but people, girls, respect. And hadn't they all given Bobby exactly that when he was the top dog? He thought they had. So, where had it all gone wrong? Hargreaves had been a rat, but Bobby was used to flushing them out. He'd been growing suspicious of 'Dickie Farrell' – Paul Hargreaves' undercover name – some time before the deal with Chilcot and Phipps. What else had changed in his life back then?... Emily! That's right. That's when it had all fallen apart. He didn't blame her – god rest her soul – but the distraction allowed him to take his mind off the game. It begged the question – wouldn't he be making the same mistake with Estela? To say he was conflicted was an understatement, at least he had plenty of miles ahead to think about it. Either way it wouldn't be a wasted trip, nor for the money he'd stashed all in his old Bristol haunts.

Bobby imagined the shock on Chilcot's face if he was spotted in that little sleepy village of Colney, he'd wake them up that was for sure. Phipps will be fuming! But not as much as Chilcot would if he realised that Phipps hadn't killed Bobby. He knew the visit would be a major risk, but he needed to say goodbye to Emily. As tempting as it would be to pay the Chilcot's a personal visit, the prospect of prison or worse made him decide a brief detour to Colney without drawing much attention was the best bet. If it did go wrong and he was spotted, then he could always overpower the geriatric Chilcot. There was also the wife; he couldn't place her exact name but remembered her well enough. That limp wasn't easy to forget, likewise her interference in his fortune. If she hadn't stuck her nose in investigating his employees then he'd have burnt Hargreaves himself, Bobby might have even kept hold of his empire. If necessary – if – Bobby would enjoy ending both of them. But Phipps couldn't know he was here, at least not until after Bobby had left the country. By then he wouldn't give a fuck what happened.

Spotting a road sign with service directions reminded Bobby's bladder, the coffee had swelled to a bursting point. He took the exit, parked the borrowed car on the far corner and entered through the restaurant. One glance, Bobby scowled at its depressed and filthy state. His greater imminent need to use the toilet outweighed any sense of pride. Bobby urgently walked in through the doors for the lavatory just as he was interrupted by a young woman, late twenties. The greasy skin and hair masked what may have been an attractive woman. He put it down to working in the sticky oiled excuse for a restaurant. Everything looked dated and broken, the staff included.

"Hi there, can I get you a seat?" she asked chewing gum. Bobby hated that.

"No, thank you, I was just hoping to use your lavatory."

"Sorry sir, the toilets are for paying customers only." He could see the look in the waitress' eyes as she took great pleasure in her shred of authority, obviously rehearsed. It's okay Bobby old chap. We don't need a scene here.

Bobby took a calming breath before continuing, "Can I have a seat please Madame?"

"Yer, but you gotta order something first. I'm not having you running to the toilet straight away and then buggering off."

What was with this girl? She could certainly do with some people skills. Bobby liked to think himself a patient man, but this was very testing indeed.

"Black coffee, is that enough?" Surely, they couldn't do that much to fuck up the coffee? It was the safest bet.

"Come on then." He held in both his bladder and anger following the girl.

"Take a seat and I'll be right over to take your order." The waitress' ritual apparently complete, Bobby made for the toilet. He let it slide that he'd quite clearly made the order already.

XXX

The toilets were a pleasant surprise. Far from perfect they had at least been treated to recent refurbishment. The facilities contrasted from the rest of the diner. If given the option, Bobby would choose this lemon-pine scented shithole to drink his coffee than the plague infested dining area. He found a fresh and vacant cubicle (being bladder shy was one of his best kept secrets. Those who were unfortunate enough to call him out on it were no longer amongst the living. Anyone else who may have had an inkling wisely kept it to themselves). And as the lock engaged, he unleashed a heavy stream into the toilet bowl and groaned in pleasure; all the annoyance he'd endured from the waitress evaporated like the yellow steam off his piss. He thought of Estela – feelings of euphoria washed over him each time. He recalled Mr Big's final moments – more euphoria still. Bobby was feeling good. He whistled his way out of the cubicle to wash his hands and whilst rubbing the soap into a lather remembered the pills in his pocket. One wouldn't hurt Bobby old chap. Best to err on the side of caution, who knew what drugs those sodomisers were using. Bobby took one of the oval shaped blue pills from the little bag turning it over to look for a marking. The tablet was plain except for its colour. Must be pharmaceutical. It went down his throat dry without water and he noticed the lack of bitterness usually associated with more potent class-A drugs. If he'd judged it right then it would be a mild buzz, a little something to enhance the car journey without losing all basic motor skills. Time would tell he supposed and with that he left the toilets.

XXX

The cacophony of clanging dinner plates quickly brought Bobby back down to reality. Patrons talking over each other and the air so thick with grease it could be cut with a knife. He was in two minds whether to sack off the coffee and make a quick exit just as the wan, worn and weary looking waitress popped up behind him.

"Thought ya tried to do a runner dint I?" she scowled, "Do you need some more time to look at the menu?"

"No." Ignoring the girl's insult of the Queen's English, Bobby took his seat, "Just a coffee. Black. No sugar."

"Not hungry then?"

He was about to turn the girl away when he noticed a customer's plate of food on the neighbouring table – black pudding! A true staple of the British diet. Bobby hadn't tasted the delicacy of congealed pigs' blood since he left for Spain. Ordinarily he wouldn't eat straight after dropping a pill but then ordinarily Bobby wouldn't drop a random unknown pill. My, how far had he fallen?

"Bacon, eggs and a couple of your black puddings my dear," Bobby chimed. It had been a long time since he'd eaten and as nobody in his near vicinity had keeled over then he guessed the food was safe for consumption. What's the worst that could happen?

"What, no beans or sausage?!" the girl asked in surprise.

Bobby was really starting to get pissed off with the waitress! Buzzing around him like a bluebottle on a pile of shit. The polite gentrified persona that he put on for such public displays slipped from his face. "Did I ask for them?"

Bobby's eyes had darkened allowing the girl to see the true horror of the twisted soul within. For a fraction of a moment she had glimpsed what this man was capable of and instinctively rubbed her throat. And like a flick of a switch it was gone. The kind smile returned, his face softened so innocent bright blue eyes shone once more. "Run along now flower," he flashed his trademark grin as the girl stumbled away to the kitchen.

The temptation to teach this urchin some respect was nearly too much for Bobby. Too much attention… too many witnesses. Maybe… if the stink of her didn't sicken him so much it would be worth the risk. But Bobby had work to do, he must focus if he was going to return to his Estela, clean of guilt, and with newfound wealth.

Bobby turned his attention back to the matter at hand. Money wouldn't be enough – he knew that now. Respect was worth more than a bag of money and that's what he was missing these days. Rebuilding a criminal empire back in England was too ambitious even for him. But why not Spain? He'd tried it before with the villagers, but the language barrier had proven too much. Perhaps with Estela's help he could teach them, or why not the orphanage itself? At least his new lover already knew the small potential army of minors, he'd have to deal with the priest first. Bobby doubted the man of the cloth would put up much of a fight. Yes. The plan had promise. He put his thoughts away for time being as the waitress peregrinated nervously towards him with his coffee and food.

"Ah! My meal has arrived." Bobby began tucking the paper napkin into his shirt collar. If he was aware of the girl's terror, then he hid it well. It was all part of the game to Bobby Cavendish. With a trembling hand she laid down the contents of the tray and left abruptly. He was pleased to see he still retained it.

Much to his pleasure, Bobby enjoyed the food. It wasn't so much of a complement to the chef as it was a result of his own poor cooking over the last half decade. Estela would change all of that. Bobby fantasised, imaging the Hispanic beauty with her head bowed slightly as she breathed in the vapours from the cooking pot. Her back to him, Bobby crept up behind taking hold of her shapely posterior pushing himself into her rump… What's all this about? The slight increase in adrenalin had been mildly noticeable to Bobby but now it was coursing through his veins down into his groin. The growing erection was insuperable. As he became more aware the feeling seemed to intensify, his skin tightened to bursting point. Bobby could feel the crotch of his tailored trousers stretching and worried for the integrity of the stitching. Fucking idiot! He now realised what the pills were. How had he not? Blue pills stolen from a queer rent boy! Of course he was aware of Viagra, but he'd never needed it. Bobby was aroused by his own power. He was his own sexual stimulant.

Nauseated by his error Bobby did the only thing he could – stay seated. Making sure that nobody was watching, he pushed a hand into the ample space left inside his boxer shorts. Discreetly as possible Bobby attempted to readjust his member, using his belt in an attempt to strap it down. His efforts were fruitless as the protruding gland muscled his trousers down below the waistline. How long does this bloody stuff last? Bobby deduced that it must have a lasting effect due to the nature of the drugs intended purpose. He couldn't sit here all day. He had work to do! It was no good, he would have to make an exit at the expense of his shame. He made a last-ditch effort to use his belt to tie the erection back to his stomach notching the belt tighter around him. Here goes nothing. He stood up from the table and beelined for the till to pay his bill.

Even Perverts Have Feelings

Following behind at his usual safe distance, Gary paused watching Jules enter the Indian restaurant. He'd never been there before; spicy food played havoc with his irritable bowel syndrome, one of many ailments. Even the aroma emanating from the eatery kitchens turned his stomach. This might be Gary's toughest stakeout yet. He would weather the storm for Jules, it would be worth it to find out who this new man was. The glass windows separating the diners from the street were tinted, thus hiding the view from his strategic vector, between two commercial dustbins. He was staring so intently at the windows, trying to make his vision beat the hued glass, that he didn't notice the curious looks from passers-by. Not that it would have made any difference to him being somewhat of an entrepreneur when it came to observing beautiful women. Gary almost believed that he could become invisible if he stood still long enough. A lady walking her dog past the bins added to his erroneous belief of invisibility by making sure not to make eye contact with the strange man and pulled the terrier away from Gary's general direction.

XXX

Any feeling had long left Gary's feet, the numbness moving up his legs by the time Jules finally emerged from the restaurant three and a half hours later. He wasn't able to enjoy the angelic look of her face as she emerged from the entrance doors. The moment was stolen from him by the short balding man who held the door open for her. Gary simmered with anger when the unknown perpetrator led Jules out into the street. The rejection was made worse by – she who should be his – linking her arm with the imposter's. Gary imagined what it would be like if he could have that arm touching his. He must have imagined a little too much because when he snapped back to reality with hand down his pants, the couple were nowhere to be seen! Bollocks. Now he wouldn't be able to follow them. Not tonight at least. That was okay – there would be other opportunities.

Gary returned to the small local authority flat which stank of mould and body cheese as a broken man. It was this kind of hurt and mistreatment by Jules that made him question if she truly deserved his attention. If she wasn't careful Gary would have to turn his affections elsewhere. She wasn't the only girl in this world, Gary fooled himself. But it was true – she hadn't always been the only girl or girls in his life. Linda had become before Jules and Donna before her. They had hurt him, but they wouldn't be hurting him now. Not anymore.

Gary stood in front of the floor to ceiling bedroom mirror admiring his naked form. He began sliding the stolen knickers up his legs squeezing himself inside of the garment before putting on the poker dot bra. A memento he'd allowed himself from Jules' flat. For someone who worked for the police she wasn't the most security conscious. He was almost too distraught over tonight's events to pleasure himself. Almost.

The Morning After

For a man who'd barely slept a wink, Austin was in a jovial mood.

So much so, he was oblivious to the frustrated and increasingly hazardous driver behind him. They flashed their headlights to inform Austin he was doing thirty-six miles an hour in a forty zone. But his mind was relaying the perfect evening he'd spent with Jules. As soon as they were seated and Mr Miah with his kindly and yet intruding staff finally left them alone, Austin's nerves had entirely dissipated! The owl dress had been the ideal conversation starter and from there, it allowed Austin to smoothly lead in with some well researched information regarding the British barn owl's diminishing numbers. The chat hadn't all been one-way traffic either. Far from it in fact, as Jules chirped in with her own knowledge on the subject. The topic moved naturally from birds to music, careers on the force and Jules' family. Austin had been evasive, but not obvious, when keeping his family life to a minimum and Jules hadn't pushed him. They'd even discussed some of the cold case he'd been working on, a new defiance of the law never before experienced by the detective constable. Jules was nothing but sympathetic to his situation involving the earlier disciplinary. He didn't think Jules could be anymore near excellence but when she revealed that she was the illusive MissSparrowhawk87 he almost gaped. After the delicious meal that neither of them could finish due to the complimentary extras Mr Miah and his staff had showered them with (Austin hadn't thought it possible to tire of onion bhajis), the lovestruck pair left the restaurant and once out the door Jules had linked her arm around his. It felt so right, so natural. Never in Austin's life had he been so complete. He wished the evening could go on and on as they walked to her apartment. And maybe it could if not for the gentleman he was. Not that it would have crossed Austin's mind to ask to come in for a 'night-cap'. Instead, Jules gave him a coy look whilst biting her bottom lip and planted the most sensual, yet slight kiss Austin had ever seen, felt or read about in any book. The night did not end there – not for him at least. His mind raced at light-speed as he tried his best to shut off and slip into sleep.

There are worse things to keep you awake at night.

Drinking in the memories gave him confidence much to the relief of the aggrieved driver behind. It gave Austin a rare sense of rebellion as he pushed the little Yaris up to an unheard of forty-two miles an hour. He made it to the station in one piece and glided through the car park into the building. Butterflies danced inside his stomach as he deliberated the best way to greet Jules. Was a kiss too much? Maybe he'd wait to see what Jules did first. Alas, it wouldn't matter what he decided as not for the first time this week Austin was about to have his bubble well and truly burst.

"Healey! In my office now!" spat a waiting Bragg.

"Sir?"

"Now Healey! I'm extending you the professional curtesy of keeping this discreet but mark my fucking words Constable, I have no qualms about airing your personal circumstances right here, right now."

Austin noticed the eyes of his colleagues watching the scene as his entire skin reddened.

"Yes sir." Like a dog with tail between legs, Austin followed the chief superintendent.

XXX

"You needn't bother taking a seat Healey. This won't take long. I want your badge and key card, as of today you are on temporary suspension."

"Why sir? I haven't even looked at the case files since you warned me." It wasn't a complete lie although he had promised to go over it with Jules later that night 'unofficially'.

"Well it would seem you've already done enough digging. I received another call from Phipps and he's warned you to back off. You don't know what you're dealing with Healey. This is big, undercover stuff that's way above your rank. If it wasn't for me sticking my neck out, you'd already be off the force."

Austin very much doubted it. There would be all manner of appeals and reviews before that was possible and he had a sneaking suspicion that Phipps wouldn't want any of that. Still, Austin could feel the tide turning against him. His career was threatening to hit rock bottom and when a man has been kicked down that low then there's not much further down you can go.

"Fuck you sir. Fuck you." Fuck! That felt great.

"I beg your fucking pardon Healey?!" Bragg's face had turned to the shade of beetroot, the veins popped out on his neck as sticky white residue foamed into the corners of his trembling mouth.

"I'm on to something. I know I am. If I have to take it further I will, but I'm not in the wrong here Chief. I will find out!" Austin chucked his badge and card down on the desk and turned his back on the palpitating man. Bragg was lost for words but managed to splutter, "Fall in line Constable. Just fall in line. Two weeks and if you keep your mouth shut I might forget about your blatant display of respect to a senior officer."

Austin walked to the door keeping his back to the chief superintendent until the last moment.

“Fuck. You. Sir.” The office echo pealed. Austin closed the door behind him.

Wherefore Art Thou Austin?

Jules' computer screen stared blankly back at her, frozen on the log in screen. The anxiety was worse than before they'd spoken to each other, it was made harder by the fact Austin was later than usual. Stupid, stupid, stupid. It seemed too good to be true. It was probably that bloody kiss! Forcing herself on him like that, she should've guessed he wasn't interested when he never asked to come into her flat. But it felt so right. At least the new dress made an impression. The young girl in the shop resembling an extra from some 'reality' show steered Jules in the direction of some very revealing outfits. In the end she'd gone with her own instincts and picked out the owl patterned dress, ignoring the girl's objections. It was the perfect conversation starter to ease both of their nerves, the newfound confidence even allowed her to reveal her online identity MissSparrowhawk87. Austin was in awe of this revelation. So where was he? Maybe she should text him? She thought it over before being drawn back to the moment by footsteps approaching her office. Only a few days had passed since Austin's reassignment to the basement, but it was enough for Jules to recognise this wasn't Austin. The detective who appeared instead holding a case file must have seen the disappointment in her face as he commented, "Who shit on your cornflakes luv?"

"What? Oh, sorry I was miles away," she managed.

"Cold case, Bragg said to bring it down and stick it with the others." She was too consumed with her thoughts to notice the detective snatching a look at her cleavage. An unusual display of flesh intended for Austin. The smarmy policeman shrugged his shoulders and made to leave the office.

"Wait!" Jules said a little too loudly.

"What's up sweet cheeks?" The detective swivelled back round to face Jules and her cleavage.

"Have you seen Detective Constable Healey today?"

The detective smirked, "Ain't you heard love? Odd nuts has been suspended. He's fucked off Bragg big time about something. Needs to learn to fall in line that one..."

The detective carried on, but Jules was no longer listening. Austin suspended? He'd told her about the cold case and how Bragg had warned him but, Suspension? Austin was on to something and if Bragg couldn't see what a talent he had, then she had a mind to put him right. That would have to wait, first she must call Austin. Jules fished the phone from her handbag noticing the detective had apparently left. The phone showed a message from Austin.

Jules. Don't worry, I've been suspended. Best you hear it from me first. Can I see you tonight?

Yours

Austin

Xxx

Ps I had a great time last night

The text had been sent twenty minutes ago. Jules chastised herself and checked the mute button on the side of her handset. Her phone was set to silent. It had happened more than a few times. Grrr. When's my upgrade due? Quickly she typed out a reply.

Oh no! Is there anything I can do?

Of course!

Last night was wonderful. I had so much fun!

Yours

Jules xxx

She hit send after reading the message through several times. Now the hardest thing to do was get through the rest of the day.

A Grave New World

The first leaves of autumn were turning yellow and crunched under foot. There hadn't been much rain yet, which made her thankful. Once they started to mulch it would make the walk to the graveyard that bit more of a challenge. Still, it was her favourite time of year even though the cold brought more pain to her ageing body. Passing by the local pub reminded her of him. It was the hub of the village, the community haven she found herself frequenting less these days. The whole village wasn't the same since he passed away nearly two years ago. A new change was coming – the time was right. The whole of Colney needed someone to fill the void left by the-great-man himself. Tears stinging her eyes, she pushed back the wrought iron gate of the churchyard and ambled to their graves. Painfully the woman bent down and cleared away the wilted flowers. They'd be replaced with fresh white lilies tomorrow – his favourite. She did the same for the girl's grave but not with as much care. It was hard not to be angry. If it wasn't for the deceased girl then he might still be alive. There was no way to be sure of course, and resentment didn't heal a broken heart. The weary woman brushed a hand over the engraving of the girl's headstone.

"Hi Hannah. I hope he's looking after you up there." She turned her focus back to her husband's grave, "Hello dear. I hope she's looking after you too," she carried on the small talk, telling her husband about the goings on in the village. "I've got some good news for you. Phipps is coming. Soon I believe. There are still a few things left to do but Martin and Fred are very excited to have a new chief. They both miss you dearly, but I think they need some guidance. Between Harry and me, we've done our best to steer them in the right direction, but neither are up to the task. Colney needs a new leader. He's earned the right for doing what you asked of him, your dying wish I suppose. See you tomorrow my darling."

With a grunting deal of effort, she stood up and limped back home.

Bad Boy

For the first time in Austin's existence he couldn't give a flying fuck. Fuck fuck fuckity fuck fuck fuck. And the use of this new word! He'd never heard himself utter it aloud before, let alone so assertedly. It was liberating. The thought had flashed through his mind that this was just a symptom of shock. Ruining your career in less than five minutes will do that, but there was something else. Why was Phipps so eager to get him away from this Hargreaves case? He wasn't ruining his career he was saving it. This was his chance to prove he possessed 'the minerals' to join Internal Affairs. Bragg couldn't keep an eye on him if he was suspended, Austin could go rogue! The very idea of it made Austin feel like a very naughty boy. Was this how it felt to break the rules? He admitted the feeling was good, but he had good reason to be. If he had to bend them, then it would be for the Greater Good of Justice.

Without the use of his station key card, Austin couldn't access the lower floors to retrieve his personal belongings. Asking Bragg wasn't an option. It would almost be worth it to see Jules. But if Bragg escorted him which was very likely, then Austin didn't want to let on they were close for her own protection. He pulled his phone out and sent a text to Jules, pausing in the car park to do so. He proofread the message at least ten times before deciding it was okay, not too desperate. Maybe one 'X' would have been enough? Well it was done now. Austin put the mobile device away and headed for his car, on the way he noticed Darren Somerville's spotlessly clean white Audi. With nothing to lose he retrieved the marmite sandwiches from his lunch box . Austin pulled apart the bread and proceeded to smear the window of his foe's car, making sure to leave some for the door handles. Fuck. That felt good. Austin was beginning to enjoy the new him.

XXX

There was never any question to what Austin would do with the rest of his day. Some may use the enforced sabbatical for some well-deserved rest or reflection. Not Austin. He arrived back at his flat and began to arrange notes whilst continuously checking his phone. There was a text from Jules which made his heart fill with joy, apparently he hadn't messed up that one. Replying instantly, they arranged to meet at Jules' flat that evening. Better still Jules promised to grab everything he'd left at the office for him. She even offered to come back from work to see if he was okay but he politely declined explaining that apart from it looking bad on her part, there were some leads to follow up. He checked the time. It was only just past ten in the morning so if he left now he could head to Colney to check the scrap yard. On his way he could drop into the roadside cafe he believed Hargreaves had visited. Austin didn't expect to find out much after five years, but it would do no harm to follow the former sergeant's last known journey.

Conducting interviews would be hard without his police ID, so he dug into his desk drawer and retrieved an old one from before he made rank as detective. It would have to do. Hopefully nobody would notice that it had expired some years before. Making his way back to the Yaris ready to hit the road, he cycled through his music library and settled on 'License to Ill' by the Beastie Boys. Once he reached the motorway, he pushed the car a little over the national speed limit. It was currently as badass as he could manage.

Tumba Poco Profunda

Father Alvaro walked the short distance to the Englishman's villa, the way was illuminated by the full moon's luminescence. Navigating the brush land like a nimble fox he made light work of the journey. The crumbling section of wall Estela had described was easy to find and despite his age, Alvaro scaled it with little effort. He set to being meticulous in staying fit, not only for himself but to set a good example to the children. He often ran several miles a day encouraging his brood to join in for as long as they could keep up.

He dropped down into the villa grounds using stealth to approach the building itself. There weren't any lights on in the property but that wasn't to mean somebody hadn't been inside sleeping. He knew only too well how easy it would be to make a mistake if he didn't employ the greatest caution. This wasn't the case for the owner of the villa as Alvaro homed in on an open window. He checked the coast was clear and hoisted himself through the opening placing his feet on a kitchen work counter. The house stunk of cleaning fluids, bleach, maybe.

Still using the moonlight flooding the house with archways in refraction. He began checking the ground floor, going room by room until he was satisfied and made for the staircase. An apprenticeship in criminal activities served him well as he silently ascended the stairs making not one creak. The upper level was abandoned just as the ground floor was. He hadn't seen any sign of Diego, the loco man or even a fight. The smell of bleach worried him, particularly as the rest of the villa lacked any basic housekeeping. Unwashed dinner plates waited in the sink, clothes had littered the master bedroom floor and disheveled bed sheets. Before he left to check the rear grounds, he walked back through to the large kitchen. He paused as the tiled slate floor ended and he felt wood under foot. Kneeling, he ran his hands along the outer edge of the planks realising there was a metal hinge attached to a trap door. A simple padlock held it closed which would be easily dismissed using the handgun, but he worried the shot would carry to the monastery. He couldn't risk alarming Estela or the other children. The girl had to stay away from the house – there was no telling what he would find beneath the hatch. Instead Alvaro silently investigated the kitchen searching for something suitable to force the lock but couldn't find anything. He had no idea what amount of time was left before the inhabitant returned so ruled out a trip back home to his own tool shed. Instead, the padre headed for the front door carefully lifting the latch and peering out into the moonlight. All was calm. With the grace of cat, he walked around the villa until he found a garage door. Luck was on his side as he tried the smaller side door and it opened easily revealing a well tooled content. Eying the workbench, Alvaro chose a pair of bolt cutters and silently returned to the kitchen ensuring he closed every door behind him. The cutters made light work of the cheap lock and he pulled the trap open revealing a wooden staircase that descended into a void of darkness. His night vision could only take him so far and he pulled out a small torch. The smell of bleach was stronger now as he made his way down into the depths, the flashlight illuminating a large tank filled with liquid in the centre of the basement. Alvaro pulled his t-shirt up over his nose to avoid inhaling the fumes that burned his nostrils and inspected the walls on all four sides. They were adorned by racks of dusty wine bottles. Along another, hanging from rusted hooks were all manner of malevolent devices that wouldn't look out of place in a medieval torcher chamber. Alvaro's stomach lurched in horror fearing for the son he'd never had. He pushed the horror away knowing that jumping to conclusions was not helpful. Walking further into the cellar flushing the shadows out with light, he found an area of ground that looked recently disturbed. The concrete and bricks had been piled haphazardly in one corner. The padre placed the torch on the floor and began to dig with his bare hands. He became more frantic clearing the rocks and digging his nails into the loose soil beneath until he touched something cold and soft. Grabbing the light from the floor he directed it at the object and let out a penetrating howl of horror. Diego's bleached white face stared out at him and suddenly all was lost. The inner beast Alvaro had worked tirelessly to control all these years boiled back to the surface and would never be tamed until he had his vengeance.

Another Pair of Eyes

Jules found it impossible to carry out her usual tasks. The worry she  endured for Austin and his career was deafening. She couldn't just sit here plowing through her usual admin duties knowing that he was out there somewhere trying to clear his name. They'd agreed to meet at her place later that night but that was an eternity from now. To clear her mind, Jules walked down the corridor to Austin's office and began clearing his desk. The distraction did her good having something of his to focus on made her feel like she was helping. Returning to her own desk Jules started to arrange his paperwork and couldn't help but scan over some of his notes. They hadn't discussed everything about the cold case last night, but he'd given her a fair idea. Deciding that it wasn't her place Jules put the paperwork aside and tried to refocus back into her usual job role, but it didn't last long. Her mind hurtling back to Austin and why Phipps was so eager to keep this seemingly uneventful case under wraps. Maybe just a quick peep. After all, she wanted to help. Against her usual good judgement Jules retrieved the cold case files. Something that could get her sacked if she was found out. The fact being – Jules was a civilian in the eyes of the law and had no right to read the files. Throwing caution to the wind, Jules ploughed on. This was for Austin. There had been a couple of moments when officers had come downstairs to drop off or collect other files but none of them seemed interested in the paperwork on her desk. So, the low-cut top had paid off after all. By the end of her working hours Jules had read the entire file and cross referenced it with Austin's own notes. Not that she expected to crack the mystery surrounding Paul Hargreaves not believing for a minute that a fine detective like Austin would have missed something. Jules was pleasantly surprised to see that he had. She double checked and then checked again – there was no doubt. Jules had stumbled upon something that she knew Austin would find very useful.

Right Direction - Wrong Road

Austin sped along. Yes. He sped along. Keeping up with the traffic, nobody flashing their lights, beeping horns or worse. He'd even gone so far as to overtake a couple of slower moving cars on the way. His community speed watch friends would be having a hissy fit. Even more so when he checked a text message from Jules. They'd been a couple already. Just checking up on him. Each one helping Austin believe – could this be real?

He parked at the infamous roadside café. The place looked busy for late September with all the summer holidays over. That was a good sign as was the run-down appearance of the outside. If it was successful and hadn't had a refurbishment, then there was a good chance it hadn't changed hands recently. It still did little to convince him he would find much of interest. But he had to start somewhere.

Walking through the front door, a blanket of heavy air laced with grease hit Austin immediately. The carpeted floor stuck to the soles of his shoes tearing like Velcro each time he took a step. Austin wouldn't choose to eat here. There was a little plastic sign on a post that had turned yellow asking customers to wait for assistance. After a short duration a waitress came to greet him.

"Table fa one yeah?"

Austin noticed she was chewing pink bubblegum. "Hello, I'm Detective Constable Healey, would it be possible to talk to your manager?" He quickly showed his old ID.

"Er… I aft ta ask dun I. Wait here," the girl took off towards the kitchen leaving Austin by the entrance. A well-dressed man except for his untucked shirt approached him. The man seemed to be in discomfort walking stiffly over to the waiting area and produced a ten-pound note. Holding it out towards Austin.

"Would you be so gracious to hand this to that charming young girl when she comes back my dear boy? Only I must hit the road. People to see you know," the man winked his blue eyes at Austin. They seemed kind.

"Yes. Of course," Austin was quite charmed by the man except for the strange way he was walking without bending his knees. Just before the gentleman reached the door, he stopped at the souvenir stand. He picked up a travel size English-Spanish book and reached back into his pocket.

"Here," he said to Austin producing another ten-pound note, "better give her that too. Thanks, old chap. The man hobbled out the door. Austin was about to ask the obviously honest and law-abiding gent if he was okay when the waitress returned.

"Did he just run off with aat payin?" She turned her head back to the kitchen taking in a deep breath to call someone, but Austin stopped her in time.

"No! No, not at all. He asked me to give you this," Austin handed over the money.

"Twenty quid! Get in! His bill was only bout seven quid. That's like thirteen quid tip or sumfin innit?" The girl's eyes lit up.

"Oh! I do apologise. He also had one of those travel books," Austin corrected.

"Well they aint that much, it's still well good. I did not see that cumin. He was proper weird, had serial killer eyes. Did you see?"

No Austin hadn't seen, far from it. Apart from being perhaps too trusting in members of the general public, Austin thought the man was nothing but courteous. And his eyes were so welcoming.

"Did you manage to talk to your manager?"

"Ah, yeah. He's not here at the minute. Don't think he's due back again today."

Austin wasn't overly surprised. But he wasn't done yet, "In that case, are there any staff who worked here about five years ago?"

"Yeah. Me," the girl's answer pleasantly surprised Austin.

"Do you mind if I ask you a few questions?"

"I'm not in trouble, am I?" she asked warily.

"Absolutely not. I'm trying to follow up on a lead about an incident reported at this establishment regarding a young boy being given a class A drug."

"Oh yeah! He was a proper weird one too. Proper pervy and that."

Austin couldn't believe his luck, "Who? Do you mean you saw the suspect who gave the boy the drugs?"

"Well, course that's circumstachel innit?" Austin knew what she meant.

"Of course, of course. But you had reason to suspect this man? I know it's been a long time, but do you think you would recognise him from a photo?"

"Well… yeah, probably."

Austin produced a photograph he'd printed out from Paul Hargreaves' file. The girl's face was unquestionable. There was bona fide disgust in her expression.

"That's him! Ah, he makes me skin crawl. Did they get im?"

"I'm afraid I'm not at liberty to discuss anything. The investigation is still ongoing. You have been a great help though thank you… sorry, what was your name?"

"Lisa."

"Thank you, Lisa. I'm Detecti…"

"Only said constable on your ID."

"Yes, do forgive me. Thank you for your time." Well played Lisa well played.

XXX

Time was still on Austin's side. If the traffic was light, then he'd make it to Colney and back in time to see Jules. He typed in the scrapyard's postcode to the sat nav and joined back onto the A303. He headed west, buoyed by the waitress' confirmation regarding Hargreaves' identity. With any luck the owners of the scrapyard where Hargreaves' car met its end, could help him further. Surely they would be more helpful in person than on the phone.

Austin made the journey in a little under two hours no thanks to the run-about his sat nav had given him. He found his destination with a mixture of persistence and a little luck. All the roads looked the same down this way. Beautiful Cotswold limestone ran on for what seemed like endless miles, but eventually he pulled into the gravel track of the metal recycling center. He guessed it must be a few miles outside of the actual village of Colney so decided another trip to the village itself would come another day – he absolutely must-see Jules tonight. The abandoned shells of vehicles lined the path up to the main building, stacked upon one another like a metallic house of cards. Austin found his way to the reception area making sure to park his car away from the metal scraps in fear of losing it to the mechanical graveyard. There was an excavator working off in the distance, but Austin noticed a light on in the reception so started there. To get to the main door he walked through a warehouse that was stacked from floor to ceiling with boxes of car parts. Each one was labelled with car makes and models as well as years of manufacture. He only had a moment to scan them but none of the boxes were labelled Lexus, the make of Hargreaves' car.

"How can I help you lovey?" The voice had come from behind Austin making him jump. There was a short heavy-set lady knocking on the door of retirement.

"Oh! Sorry you surprised me. I believe we've talked on the telephone. I'm Detective Constable Austin Healey. I made the enquiry concerning the Lexus."

"Yes! The bloke with a car for his name, although I could swear it was Morris Minor. So, you fancied a trip to our little quarter did you Officer?"

"I suppose you'd be right there Mrs McKay. And yes, it is unquestionably Austin Healey."

"Well, how can I be of use to you? I thought we told you everything on the telephone?"

"No. Not really Mrs McKay. I was still wondering if you had any of the car left here at all? I see you have many buckets filled with various car parts. I don't suppose you would have any of the Lexus in question?" Austin knew it was unlikely he'd find out anything new but then he'd been wrong about the diner.

"I'm afraid not dear. You see, we don't get many of them come through here. Parts like that are rare as rocking horse shit, my husband would tell you as much."

"Is your husband around Mrs McKay? I would like to speak to him if possible."

"Oh my poor love, you've just missed him! He went out to collect an accident recovery."

How convenient thought Austin. He was tempted to push the point and ask who was driving the excavator, but another thought came to him, "Mrs McKay, you mentioned that it was your brother in law's tractor that came into contact with the Lexus. Would I be able to ask for his address as I've come all this way?"

"You could my flower, but I'm afraid it won't do you much good. He's gone with his brother to collect the accident recovery."

Hmmm. Another convenience that didn't sit right with Austin. It wasn't lost on him that the woman still hadn't given him an address. There was definitely something the lady was hiding. But today wasn't the day to push it further. Austin would have to return another time when he didn't have the beautiful Jules waiting at home. Maybe he'd book a room in Colney itself? Make a couple of days of it. Much harder for people to allude him that way.

"You could always visit our local police force in Colney village Officer? I'm sure they would be only too happy to assist you further?" Austin had the feeling that this was more of a threat than a helpful suggestion. It would be wise to tread carefully around the local police, not only for the mystery surrounding DCI Chilcot's involvement but also to not alert Phipps or Bragg to his continued investigation.

"Okay Mrs McKay. Perhaps I'll be more fortunate on my next visit. If you or Mr McKay think of anything else, please don't hesitate to contact me."

"Of course, dear. We have your number." Austin doubted she still did and didn't see any calls coming his way. He nodded at the rotund lady and headed back to his car.

***

Mrs McKay watched the Toyota Yaris disappear down the gravel path. She waited until it was firmly out of view before waving over to the distant excavator. A short but well-built man leapt from the cab and made his way over. He arrived by his wife's side as she continued to stare down the pathway.

"Was that him?" he gasped out of breath from the distance he covered in a short time.

"Yes. I don't think he's going to leave it Jon. It's time we made a call."

"Okay my love. I'll call Alice."

A Slight Return

Ridding himself of the stagnant café though not the raging erection, 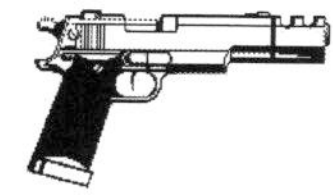 Bobby wondered if a slight change in plan was necessary. Turning up to his would-be widow's grave may be a slight disrespectful given his temporary mutation. He'd booked a return from Gatwick, so it made no difference to his journey what way around he arranged his business. Being the romantic he was, Bobby couldn't trust the visit to his once beloved Emily – Hannah – whatever – wouldn't turn him soft. He had to be totally focused when returning to Bristol. As long as his hiding place still existed and hadn't been built over by the ever-expanding city then he wouldn't need much time. Gaining access wouldn't be easy and may take a great deal of hard exterior. Intimidation was so much easier when you had two giant wrestlers for back up. Bobby hadn't started his empire with anyone but himself, he still possessed the skills to be persuasive without anybody else's help. The last known stash of money from the Bobby Cavendish empire was buried beneath a thin concrete floor. This floor was inside an old lock-up on the outskirts of the city. Only two men knew of the hiding place – Bobby Cavendish and Paul Hargreaves. Only one man still lived. Bobby had been close to sharing the information with Phipps when the police chief had visited him some years earlier in Spain. And perhaps if it wasn't for Emily then Bobby would have. It would have been a safer bet than coming back himself, but he could no longer risk trusting Phipps. After all, hadn't Phipps deceived his one-time mentor the great DCI Chilcot? Not only that but Phipps had been sent to kill Bobby by the 'holier than thou' Chilcot. If it hadn't been for the then multiple amounts of contingency money, then Bobby was far too aware how differently things could have turned out. How dare Chilcot try to renegade on the deal! It would be almost worth the risk to knock on the old man's door right now, his impatience bubbling to the surface before he composed himself. For now – Bristol. The plan made sense seeing as it was likely the Chilcot's would sound the alarm if they saw him. He reasoned they would probably be too busy questioning Phipps why the man they'd sent him to kill was visiting their niece's grave. Interestingly Phipps had brought up the idea of the pay-off to Bobby himself. Both men were lucky that there had been some money, or the situation could have ended very differently for both of them. Bobby liked to believe he would have come off the better of the pair. All this thinking of revenge hadn't helped to stem the flow of blood to his manhood. If he was to shake the disability it had to be clean thoughts from now on – methodical thinking and planning was what was needed. Oh, but my Estela! Within an instant the juices began to flow back to his penis. NO. Concentrate Bobby old chap!

XXX

An hour later Bobby's concentration had got the better of him. So much that he pulled over into an unoccupied lay-by, forced to literally take matters into his own hands. It hadn't taken him all that long, a surprise to Bobby as he thought that the idea of the drug was to prolong sex. He found some wet wipes in the inside of Mr Big's Jag and mopped up. Bobby was relieved in more ways than one until after barely pulling away from the parking spot, the erection returned. Still, it lost some of its fight which was something he supposed. Traffic depending, he should arrive at the lock-up in a little over an hour. Hopefully it would subside by then.

Precisely one-hour and forty-two minutes later Bobby arrived in the little industrial estate. He'd stopped one more time to 'exercise' more demons from his loins but now the feeling had thankfully worn off except the odd spasm. He was also delayed by the necessity to stop at a well-known DIY store on his way to purchase bolt cutters, a lump hammer and a bolster. To his relief the estate seemed quiet and deserted which emboldened Bobby to park directly outside the brick-built buildings. At least he wouldn't have to deal with anyone – he was slightly disappointed. A new looking chain and padlock were wrapped around the swinging door handle linking it to a well secured hook on the ground. Fortunately, the bolt cutters made quick work of the cheap metal and Bobby opened up the doors revealing a stunning sight that threatened an explosion from Bobby's already exhausted bollocks. It was a cherry red classic Mercedes in mint condition. Not just any 'Mercedes' but a 1969 Mercedes-Benz 280SL. Bobby had owned one before taking leave from his Bristol empire, a thought came to him that it could in fact be his but that would have been too much of a coincidence. On closer inspection he could see other dissimilarities from his own not to mention the colour itself. He'd always thought red a bit too much of a feminine look but now seeing the gorgeous machine he was wondering if he'd got that one wrong after all. Bobby had planned on ditching the Jaguar as it was – someone was bound to discover Mr Big at some point. Never in his wildest dreams did he imagine such an upgrade. Admittedly it wasn't the most inconspicuous car for a man trying to be incognito but, Bobby was on holiday. Take it, take it. Bobby's inner voice winning him over. First things first! The car was a tight fit in the garage but there was still a pathway around to the back of the small space where he buried the money some years before. He pulled the garage door shut finding a convenient torch on the worktable and began breaking up the concrete floor. The patch he had to get at was covered by a small inch of screed and only a foot or two wide. Under the concrete was a layer of plywood that he could pull away revealing a crevice with the bag inside. Bobby had struggled and cursed a few years earlier when making the hiding place with his own hands, such was his lack of manual labour. Usually he would have one of his many employees to do such work, but this had to be his secret and his alone. The unskilled job paid off in the end as he made quick work with the loose concrete layer. Retrieving the bag, he turned his focus to the Merc. Now this was more his skillset – Bobby had built his early career on carjacking and knew all too well how easy it was in a car of its vintage age. The battery was predictably dead, but he saw jump cables on the bench and pulled the Jag up to the garage. After a small confusion of where to peg the neutral crocodile clip on the Jag's engine, Bobby fired up the old Mercedes with a fill of excitement. She purred like a tiger. He swapped the cars over and poured the contents of a petrol can over Mr Big's Jag, he wouldn't be leaving any chance DNA behind. He wiped the outer garage door and chain clean with one of Mr Big's baby-wipes before flicking the cigarette lighter from the Mercedes console towards the garage. The flames began to lick around the Jag catching up higher until black smoke poured from the lock-up. Satisfied that the visit couldn't have gone any better, Bobby stamped on the accelerator. He had one more person to see. Trying to board an airplane with three-quarters of a million-pounds wouldn't go down well with customs. Bobby hadn't dropped everybody in the shit for his deal with Chilcot and Phipps, and 'Wookie the Bookie' was one such fellow. Bobby always had time for Wookie.

Eight years earlier – Bristol

Bobby walked downstairs from the office above Blue Tiger strip club. He wasn't quite sure what he was about to walk into but "Boss you better come and see this" normally meant bad news. He finished the descent leaving the spiral staircase for the private door into the 'performance' area. This was the main part of the club. There were three different stages throughout the space, a bar ran along one wall and the doors to the 'private' rooms took up two of the others. It didn't take Bobby long to work out which room was of concern. He knew from the CCTV that one of his girls, Sarah, had taken a man in a few minutes before. The man was of good stock, he'd set up one of those online betting sites. Bobby couldn't remember the man's name but possessed everything upstairs on every customer and every staff member who came through his doors. This gentleman matched Bobby's criteria of the customer he usually liked. He always dressed well, spent a lot and most importantly… he had respect! He'd watched the man as he did everyone who came into his club and quickly became satisfied with the way he carried himself. So, what had gone wrong tonight? Bobby walked the room, parting the manifesting crowd of onlookers like Moses. The growing number of people trying to get a look at the audible distress coming from the private room were a mix of customers and employees. He made a mental note to remove a finger of the individual who had stopped the music.

"Lionel!" The beast of a man moved with defiant grace, dropping in at his Boss' side. "Ask our paying customers if they would 'like' to make their way to the function room. Offer them a complimentary glass of champagne and ask Michelle to put on a special show. Tell her I know I'm asking a lot of her, but she can pick the other girl. She gives you any resistance Lionel, tell her she'll be finding her drugs somewhere else. Ha! Good luck with that! And tell everyone else to get back to work."

"Yes Boss."

"And one more thing Lionel. Find that prick who turned off the music."

By the time Lionel had begun barking orders at everybody the room had almost cleared. Bobby saw that his man Brian Crosson had taken control of whatever was beyond the blocked doorway. Four of his girls and a couple of other well-dressed men waited around the doorway.

"Girls, get back to work. You heard Lionel. Don't test me."

The strippers, although worried about the fate of their colleague decided they would rather not be on the end of worse and walked away. Bobby watched them leave. You've good a good eye for an arse Bobby! His top boy Crosson saw Bobby through the slightly open doorway.

"Boss. You need to come see this."

"So I hear Brian. So I hear." Bobby waltzed passed the two stragglers. The customer's entourage. One of them in a turtleneck made a move towards Bobby which ordinarily would have been met with deadly resistance – except – the man was in a turtleneck. Bobby let him speak.

"Please Mr Cavendish, sir. Wookie wouldn't have done anything on purpose. He's a good guy!"

Bobby motioned to his other trusted soldier, "Get these boys home Joe." He liked the manners of the lad. "Don't worry about your friend here. We take care of our customers. Joe is going to give you a lift home. On the way he will tell you about the last time anybody got themselves a loose tongue. I'm sure you understand?"

"Yes Mr Cavendish!" the boys replied in unison. Bobby liked these two.

"Good boys… I hope this won't deter you from visiting us again?"

"No Mr Cavendish!" again, together.

"Then please allow my good friend to escort you home for the night. He looks mean but I assure you – Joe has the most beautiful soul of any man I've ever met… Just don't piss him off!" Bobby and Joe exchanged a mischievous look before Joe glared at the two young men.

“Home. Now.” They both followed Joe without hesitation.

Bobby walked into the room. It was obvious. Sarah was dead.

In the corner of the room Brian Crosson tried to calm the man Bobby had watched from the cameras. Bobby looked at the naked and sobbing mess and learnt his nickname exceeded the ginger hipster, hair and beard – would’ve been alright if not for that fucking topknot! He was covered in hair head-to-toe. But what really took his attention was the size! The length. The girth of the bloody thing! It was monumental. The man’s penis belonged in an Amsterdam art gallery.

“What do we have here Brian? And don’t bloody tell me ‘that’ is the murder weapon!” Bobby laughed at his own joke – a lot.

“Actually Boss. It is. Luke ‘Wookie’ Chambers here suffocated Sarah. Now I’m in the mind that’s he’s telling the truth Boss. I mean, you’ve seen the size of the thing!”

Bobby walked over to the well-hung sniveling mess “What happened Luke? Now, I’m a fair man, but give me any bullshit and things won’t end well for you here.”

Luke sniffed and cleared his snotty throat, “She was just giving me head Mr Cavendish. I don’t know what happened after that… she just sought of stopped… I'm so sorry Mr Cavendish," Luke choked back sobs, but he seemed to feel better getting things off his chest.

Brian stepped in, "The lads outside said they were all in here Boss. Apparently, she'd been going down on all of them but when Dirk Diggler over here got his go, things took a bit of a turn for the worse."

"Well I can see that Brian!" Bobby laughed. If he was distressed by the death of one of his girls then he wasn't showing it.

"Question is, what are we going to do about this mess… Wookie? I mean you can't just go around suffocating the staff with your massive fucking cock, can you?"

"No Mr Cavendish. I'm so sorry Mr Cavendish. I'll do anything. Pay anything, just please don't kill me!" Wookie collapsed back into his snotty heap.

"Well, what can you do for me Mr Wookie? What's this business you run?"

The hairy man seemed to compose himself with these words. He was beginning to sense there may be a way out of this. He knew he'd fucked up, even the lads had told him to let the girl breathe, but he was so close. All he'd needed was another second and he'd of been done. Wookie rubbed his furry arms over his face, trying to make himself more presentable.

"I run an online gambling site. I'm sure we can work something out, I don't want to speak out of turn Mr Cavendish sir, but I can turn cash into currency without turning any heads."

Bobby rubbed his chin thinking it over. Yes, he had people on the payroll who could offer similar services, but Bobby always liked to have options and this man was firmly in his pocket – his wildcard. Luke 'Wookie' Chambers was certainly more of an asset than the girl had been. They could be replaced.

"Well it looks like we have a deal Mr Chambers," Bobby extended his hand to the man, helping him to his feet, "Just keep that bloody thing on a leash next time you come in here son!"

"Yes, yes of course. Thank you, Mr Cavendish. I won't let you down."

"No, I don't suppose you will. Now, get your clothes on and wait for Joe. He'll take you home. I'll be seeing you again. Can't tell you when, but when I need you, you'll know about it."

Bobby left the room and the devastation within. Brian knew what to do – they were well rehearsed for this type of thing. He made a mental note to install CCTV in all of the rooms from now on.

XXX

When Bobby had made that deal, he'd no idea it would be so long before he pulled Wookie up on it. Naturally the man had assumed his debt wiped due to Bobby's alleged death, but to his credit he kept his word. Bobby was right to trust him, although he'd been slightly nervous handing his bag over to a stranger in a car park not far from the outskirts of Bristol. When he checked his bank balance, he saw that the man had come through. There was only one thing left on his agenda – Emily here I come!

Bait

"…and for that dramatic decrease in crime I thank all of the police

officers involved. I have been humbled and honored to lead the Avon and Summerset police-force, some of the brightest officers in the country I must add. But with heavy heart I am announcing my retirement from the police service."

Chief Constable Phipps carried on talking to the cameras, thanking colleagues who had helped over the years. It was all very scripted but then it hadn't been his idea. The public relations department thought it would be good PR, especially as it followed some rather underwhelming crime figures. Phipps' reputation was still good with the public eye thanks to his Bristol days leading the way in ending Bobby Cavendish's reign of terror. It was laughable, His dramatic rise in the force was based on an entire lie and he'd failed to make good on Cavendish's death when handed a second chance. He couldn't regret that, the money he'd reclaimed for Bobby had been life changing.

Phipps finished his speech and exchanged pleasantries with the film crew. Diane Farrow from PR swooped in beside him, clipboard in hand.

"That was really great Chief Constable. Really sincere. Yes, it looks good on us to have you make a public announcement."

“Thanks Diane.” Phipps was already reaching in his jacket pocket for the phone. He didn’t really care anymore. He was done with it all. All he wanted now was his cushy paid retirement in sleepy Colney – the job was all but his.

“And Sir?”

“Yes Diane?”

“It’s been an honor,” Diane held out her hand clutching her clipboard awkwardly. The gesture clearly meant a lot to the woman. Phipps paused for a second his eyes scrutinising the open hand then extended his own.

“Thank you, Diane. Same to you. All the best.” Diane dropped her head nervously and scuttled off. Phipps had sworn the woman couldn’t stand him.

He left the headquarters and headed for his car. Not for the last time, the statement was for the public only. Phipps still had work to finish before his replacement arrived. He started his car engine and turned his phone on. A flurry of message alerts flooded the screen, nothing worth much of note except one missed call – Alice Chilcot. Phipps didn’t hesitate, excitedly returning the call. No doubt this was his long-awaited confirmation in becoming Colney’s newest ‘Police Chief’.

“Hello Alan. I’m glad you could return my call,” Alice Chilcot’s voice answered without a hint of emotion.

“Hello Alice, I do hope you are well. What do I owe the pleasure?” Phipps crossed his fingers.

“As well as can be Alan. Today’s always the hardest for me. You understand I’m sure.”

Shit! He’d almost forgotten.

“Yes, of course Alice. I send all of my love and support to you all… I hope I can be there in person for you soon.” Was that a bit too much? He hadn’t meant to be that obvious.

“I’m sure you would Alan.” Phipps didn’t think that sounded too promising. I’ve given my bloody job up now for fucks sake! Why does she keep hanging it out? Chilcot promised!

“But I still have him,” Alice added after the slight pause.

“Yes. Yes, of course Alice. We all do. Yes. We all do…” Phipps trailed off confused as to what the conversation was all about.

“Alan. We have a problem. There’s an outsider claiming to be a police officer asking too many questions. The things he’s asking about involve all of us Alan.”

Rolling his eyes, Phipps silently cursed Bragg for his failure to control this bloody… Austin-fucking-Healey. This guy was really pushing his buttons now, Phipps had no choice. This Austin fellow really had done it to himself. Sniffing around Phipps was one thing – but this Colney lot were a different breed altogether and now Austin-fucking-Healey had walked right into their web. Phipps wasn't really into the whole Wicker-Man-Scarecrow thing, but it would do his reputation in the community no end of good.

"Austin Healey, I presume?" he replied.

"Yes, that's him. Do you mean to tell me you're already aware that he's onto us and not bothered to warn me?" Alice spat with venom.

"Alice, please listen. His name has come up, he's been looking into a cold case that he's convinced himself crosses over onto one of my undercover officers, but I assure you he's not a threat. I'm on top of this."

"And would that officer be Sergeant Paul Hargreaves by any chance? Do you think I'm a fucking idiot Phipps? This policeman has been looking for Hargreaves' car. He's on to something. He told Betty McKay he was coming back to speak to Charlie! My Husband!"

"It's okay Alice, please, trust me. I think we've overlooked what an opportunity this is."

"How do you mean Alan?"

"You know what I mean Alice. He could be my first, this could be my offering," Phipps was bouncing with adrenalin. He wasn't usually that sort of bloke but the idea of everyone hailing him as their new saviour reminded him of a younger Alan Phipps.

"We have to approve you as our new protector first Alan. Anything else would just be murder," Alice said this last part with conviction.

"But what if you all helped me? I mean no crime is done until the last act. Help me trap him and I can prove myself before the festival's end?" A win, win for everyone – surely.

"..." The line stayed that way for some time apart from the audible sound of each other's breathing. Finally, Alice replied, "...Okay. Can you get him here?"

"Yes." It wouldn't be hard. He'd call Austin straight away and give the young officer exactly what he wanted – the truth... and death. Oh yes. There would definitely be some dying involved.

Aegypius Monachus

Gary waited in his favourite hiding place. There was a narrow alley between two of Jules' neighbouring flat blocks and Gary really had made it his own. That was apart from the odd mangey cat rubbing itself up against his tracksuit bottoms. He kicked the cat away – the velour trousers were fresh on this morning. Gary was hoping to make a good impression on Jules today, he was going all out. He watched from his hiding spot as Jules returned from work punctual as ever. The look on her beautiful face had been one of deep concentration Gary noticed. It was different from the one of nerves and excitement he'd witnessed the day before. He did hope she was okay. This new man – NO – imposter had better not have hurt his sweet princess. Gary was only kidding himself; he really hoped the man had done exactly that. He knew from experience that a woman was at her most vulnerable after a broken heart and he would be there ready to swoop in like a vulture.

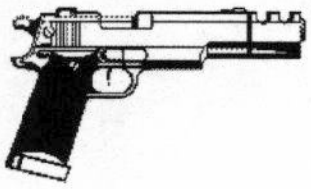

Jules' blinds opened for just a moment – the second window on the right-third floor up. For an instant, Gary soaked in the glorious sight – behold! Jules waved at someone on the street before closing the blinds again. Gary poked his head out of the makeshift lair tracing his head in the direction Jules had been looking. It was him! The devil himself, sleuthing at a steady pace towards her sacred sanctum. She won't invite him inside.

That was for him only. He wasn't worried. That was until the stranger waited at the main door and not only did Jules not appear to meet the visitor, but the man walked straight inside. Surely she hasn't let him! Gary was convinced the man somehow tricked his way past the security door. She wouldn't let him in. He almost toyed with the idea of calling the police but with Gary's past record it might reflect badly on him. One thing was for sure – Gary was in for a long shift tonight. Thankfully he'd brought a second flask of tea.

Mating Season

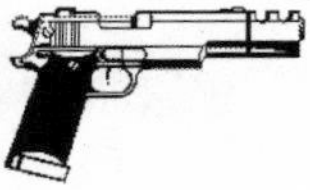

The drive home from Colney had been uneventful. Austin was able to return his focus to the delightful Jules. He was back through his door with more than enough time to get ready – if Austin was honest with himself, another week wouldn't have been enough time to polish a turd. He arrived at Jules' block of flats shortly before seven. He noted that the neighbourhood was quiet with not many people around apart from a strange homeless looking man poking out from the alley. As Austin walked towards the block Jules had given him the address for, a set of blinds opened in one of the windows revealing the radiant site of Jules waving directly at him. Austin's heart did somersaults as was now the standard feeling that she evoked within. He waved back – not too much he hoped as he pictured himself as one of the manic waving contestants on a million-pound-quiz-show. The buzzing of the security door let Austin know that he was welcome. He walked into the modern vestibule and found his way to the lift. Everything about the place screamed modern and clean, a far cry from his drab and worn converted townhouse. Clearly Jules had taste. Oh well, Austin could learn he told himself whilst locating the correct door. He didn't have to try hard as Jules was standing with the door open. Austin barely uttered the word 'hello' before Jules grabbed him for a loving embrace. Austin breathed in the woman's heavenly scent, a mix of strawberries and freshly baked biscuits!

"Wow!" was all he could muster.

"Oh, no! Was it too much? I knew it was too much. Sorry, I've just been so worried about you," Jules chastised herself.

"No. No. No, not at all. I loved it." Did he really just say 'loved'? But it was true, he had. And it couldn't ever be too much. Ever.

Jules ushered him in closing the door as they made small talk, picking up just as they had the night before. All the nerves between them diminishing like a cloud of dissipating vapor. Austin commented on the unique style of the flat, Jules' décor and the surrounding area. She asked about Austin's journey and he filled her in careful not to leave out one detail.

"So that's when I left the scrapyard, but I know there's more going on there. At least the waitress could ID Hargreaves for me. It wasn't a complete waste of time but unfortunately, I am left with the prospect of another trip to Colney. I must admit, I've even considered dropping the whole thing like Bragg said. I feel a bit lost without my badge and if my fake one was noticed by the waitress then I doubt it will be much use with

Colney's own police force, especially if this DCI Chilcot lives up to reputation."

Jules had listened to Austin with chills of excitement, not wanting to interrupt but furtively enjoying the suspense. She was about to blow his world and it wouldn't be the last time tonight.

"Austin… I've got something to tell you. Please don't be angry with me, I couldn't just sit there doing Bragg's bidding whilst you were off saving your career and upholding justice. I… I looked at your notes… And the case file."

"Jules! That's strictly against the law for civilians to access those types of record without supervision. You could lose your job or worse!" He wasn't that angry about her flaunting the law but what if she'd been caught. Austin was a changing man but that was too much for one day.

"I know! Austin I'm so sorry but you need to take a look at what I found," Jules felt like she was losing the moment, it was imperative she made Austin listen. She grabbed some papers from the coffee table and thrust them into Austin's hands before he could protest, "Just look… Paul Hargreaves' money from the sale of his house in London was passed to a trustee. I checked with the solicitors who forwarded me a copy of the details they sent some years before. Another officer had requested they be sent to him directly, they accepted as Hargreaves had given this individual power of attorney over his assets. That officer was the formerly ranked Chief Superintendent Alan Phipps," Jules paused for breath – she wasn't done yet. Austin meanwhile stared dumfounded at the papers in his hand, his brain struggling to process the information whilst also wondering how he hadn't thought to check with the solicitors himself. Jules used the silence to draw air into her lungs and quickly continued.

"And it doesn't just end there. Phipps then used the money to buy a villa in Spain in Hargreaves' name. The address is…" she rummaged through some more papers on the table before finding the right one, "let me see… there, this one!"

Jules held out the evidence expecting Austin to take it, but he just stood there motionless his eyes glazed. Stupid girl! You've broken him.

"Austin?" She clasped her hands around his shoulders and shook him back to normality.

"What? Oh… er… sorry Jules."

"Are you okay Austin? I'm sorry if I went too far and I know it isn't anything you wouldn't have worked out for yourself. I was just hoping I could help you in some way."

The problem was Austin didn't think he would have worked it out himself. Did that make him a failure? Did it matter? This beautiful, intelligent and courageous woman had taken a huge risk to her own career and freedom to help him. Was there anything else that mattered more than that? Was this love? He looked into her welcoming brown eyes and a smile spread across his face.

"Jules. I could kiss you!"

"Then what's stopping you?" They wrapped their arms and then lips around each other in unison.

XXX

The evening's meal had burnt in the oven beyond any human consumption. The smell of which was the only thing that pulled Jules out of Austin's arms. He watched her naked and lithe body leave the bed as she headed to the kitchen, grabbing a dressing gown on the way. Austin had just experienced the best seventeen minutes of his entire life. There was none of the awkwardness from his first sexual encounter. The two of them had melted into one another. If it hadn't been for the acrid smoke they may have never moved again. Jules was more than competent, not that Austin had much prior experience to compare it to but the way she had taken him in her mouth suggested that it wasn't her first time. The observation hadn't bothered Austin at the time and probably wouldn't again – unless he was given too much time to think about it – on say, an international flight to Spain.

Jules returned back to the bedroom. Austin looked up at her perfectly formed face. “Need any help?” he asked whilst trying to locate his boxing shorts.

“I think you’ve done enough Detective,” Jules purred at him before allowing the dressing gown to drop off her body and climbed back on top of him. They enjoyed another twenty-two minutes of bliss – Austin was smashing his own records tonight.

XXX

After what should have been an eternity but was torn apart by both their physical hunger, Jules and Austin dressed and sat on the sofa together. As they waited for the pizza delivery to attune for the cremated oven, they went back over all the information. A trip to Spain was in the investigation’s best interest. If Austin could prove that Phipps was up to something or better yet, speak with the missing Hargreaves then he may even be able to get his badge back. It would be too risky going to Colney without the weight of the law behind him. After the damning evidence on Phipps’ part, it was hard not to wonder if Hargreaves had in fact himself stumbled upon some wrongdoing of his former boss. Austin would exercise extreme caution in Spain. Jules booked his flight and hotel so as not to raise suspicion from his seniors. It would look like a well needed bit of R&R after his recent suspension. Naturally Jules worried about him and offered to come but Austin thought it too dangerous. After tonight he wanted to protect her more than anything. The hardest part was tearing himself away from Jules, but somehow, he knew she would be there when he got back. It was real.

Preparation is the Key

It had taken the rest of the night to dig a proper grave for Diego.

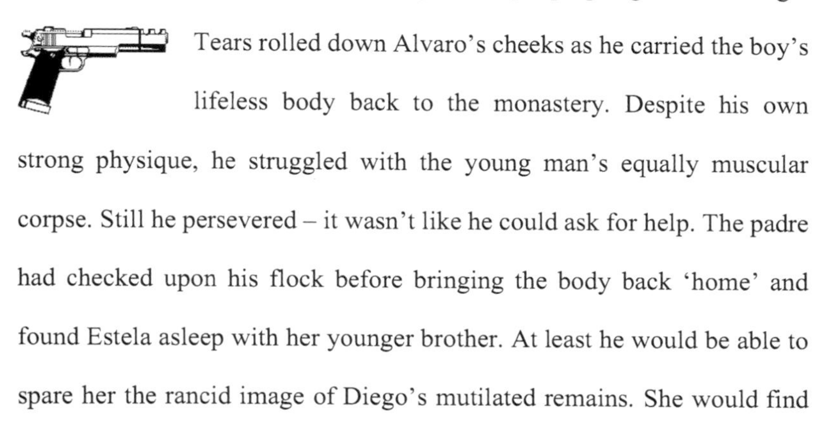

Tears rolled down Alvaro's cheeks as he carried the boy's lifeless body back to the monastery. Despite his own strong physique, he struggled with the young man's equally muscular corpse. Still he persevered – it wasn't like he could ask for help. The padre had checked upon his flock before bringing the body back 'home' and found Estela asleep with her younger brother. At least he would be able to spare her the rancid image of Diego's mutilated remains. She would find no closure from such a sight.

The sun was making its first stretches into the day; he finished pouring the soil over his prodigy's final resting place. Alvaro could feel his ageing body yearning for sleep. It was too tempting to lay his head down before the children woke up, but he knew once he gave in, he wouldn't wake for some hours. He couldn't risk Estela finding the fresh grave, or worse returning to the villa before he could speak with her. Today was going to be a very long day for Alvaro and breaking the news to Estela was only the beginning.

The sound of the old, swollen, heavy door stirred Estela awake. She shushed her little brother back to sleep as she stood up from the little bed and stretched. It was still dark outside as the recollection of the evening before came flooding back, and with it, the realisation that sleep was no longer possible. Estela walked within the inhabited part of the former holy residence. Coffee would cleanse the cobweb-curtain of sleep, she entered the kitchen. The kettle boiled as she stared through the window at the sun in its first impressions upon morning and with it – the silhouette of a man working in the graveyard. Padre! A sick feeling lurched her stomach as she dropped and shattered the coffee cup and its black contents. Estela ran out of the building, her mind tumbling, closing in on the now visible Alvaro.

"Padre! What are you doing? No! Don't say it is him!" She collapsed to her knees sobbing with her head in hands. Alvaro as shocked as he was at Estela's unexpected arrival – yet still relieved she hadn't been twenty minutes earlier – reached down to hold the girl's shoulders with affection. He lowered himself down to her level taking her in his arms letting the girl sob into his sweat soaked shirt. "It's okay. He's at peace now Estela. It's okay." Alvaro, now as the universe collapsed in upon itself, couldn't hold his own convulsions anymore. They stayed that way until the sun was firmly in the sky. He would have stayed longer if not for the needs of the other children. He finally broke away from the distraught girl's embrace. "I must see to the others Estela. Will you be okay here?" She nodded her head before a further crescendo of wailing erupted. Alvaro forced himself away from the broken girl. He would have his revenge – the sweet innocent child had suffered enough in her short life – he'd sworn to protect her ever since she'd entrusted him with her secret past. Subtly hidden from Estela, Alvaro had taken a trip a few years back to the city where her mother lived. The vile woman, and her equally fowl lover, had begged for his mercy and in Alvaro's way – he had been only too willing to relieve the pair of their sins.

Before he reached the main building Estela shouted with a shaking voice, "Where is he Padre? Where is the fucker who did this?!" He didn't have the answer she wanted, he would soon.

"Wait for me here Estela… promise me!"

"Where? Where is he Padre? I want to kill him my-fucking-self!" Alvaro knew the stages of grief well. He'd seen it all before, soon there would be bargaining in the image of guilt. It was this stage of anger that he would need to draw upon for himself first. It was all he could do to keep the guilt at bay – for now at least.

"Wait for me Estela."

"Promise me Padre. Promise me we will kill him."

Never had he been so confident of keeping a promise in his life, but the girl – she didn't need this. Still so pure and innocent, he didn't want to destroy it. Alvaro knew that there would be no coming back from this, but he also knew that she wouldn't let him go alone. Not now. There were ways she could help him without actually doing the macabre task itself. He would make sure she was nowhere near when that happened.

"Wait for me Estela. We have much to do." Alvaro headed inside leaving the girl to pay her final respects.

Alvaro went to see the rest of the children and delegated the tasks for the day ahead to them accordingly of age and capabilities. Mikel was the next eldest to Estela and Diego, perhaps not at the level of maturity but he was a good boy – the natural choice to be left with the responsibility of running things while he and Estela returned to the villa.

XXX

Estela's tears had been replaced with anger and endless questions. Most of them he answered honestly but others he just didn't have the answer for. The one question he really cared about was when the loco man would return. Alvaro pushed back the nagging worry that maybe the man was never going to return, but he couldn't let himself believe that right now. The man was pure arrogance and men like that always returned to the scene of their crime – Alvaro would be waiting. He managed to get Estela to reluctantly wait for him, checked the villa was still empty, what had taken him half the time in the daylight. Satisfied that the coast was clear, he returned for the girl to begin the work. He was worried that it was too much for her to start with as she looked around the villa her tears threatening to burst the damn she'd built.

"You do not need to be here Estela. There is no weakness in going back to be with the others, Diego wouldn't want you to suffer this way," he tried offering her the chance to back out, but she wasn't having any of it, "No Padre. I must do this and you're wrong, Diego would do this for me. I must honour him."

"Okay, but it needs to be done right." Alvaro looked around the building making calculations in his head, "Do you have the sheets?" Estela nodded and started pulling them from the stuffed bags they'd brought from the monastery. "Then let us begin, but Estela, you must promise me you will go all the way back home and wait. Under no circumstances do you come back here until I say so."

"But Padre, what ab…"

"No Estela! You must do as I say and then I will sit down with you and explain everything about me." And he knew that this time he would.

"But how will I know if you're okay? How will I know if it's done?"

"You will know Estela. The whole village will know. You are to tell the children that padre is out hunting wild game, that way they will not fear the gunshots. Now, quickly! We have to get to work." As Estela helped

Alvaro spread out the old bedsheets, she couldn't help but worry – what if Padre wasn't the only one with a gun?

Back from the Grave

The moon was rising to mark the beginning of night so Bobby flicked the lights on. He easily located the switch on the car, such was his familiarity with the model. The drive south had been majestic! Much to his relief, the earlier erection had completely subsided. There was no denying that the experience had drained him, both physically and mentally. He started to keep an eye out for somewhere to sleep for the night, it was pointless turning up to a graveyard to pay your last respects to the former love of your life in pitch darkness. The classic car sped past a motorway motel – not for Bobby. He'd been happy to use the one from last night but then Bobby hadn't been paying. No. Bobby Cavendish could afford something much more lavish. A sign flashed past advertising a country golf course hotel. Now that was more suited to a man of his status! Bobby counted down the miles and followed the signage until he arrived at the lavish property's front gates. He drove up the gravel pathway which snaked this way and that over greens that seemed to stretch for miles. Finally, he arrived at the hotel itself. The white four-story building with pillars each side of the front door screamed money, something Bobby now had in abundance. Yes. This was the one. He'd have to be gone early, the plane flight was booked for the following afternoon and he had a lot of ground to make up. Bobby let the valet take his borrowed car – the vintage Mercedes may attract too much unwanted attention after today. It was with regret that he wouldn't be leaving in it. On the flip side he realised how easy it would be to exchange for a new one right here. With the small fortune it cost to stay at the hotel, nobody expected anybody to steal anything.

Bobby booked in at reception taking his key and heading straight to his room. It was still early evening, but he didn't struggle to sleep.

Estela danced barefoot on the sandy beach laughing merely at life itself. Bobby watched her while sucking on a cold bottle of suds – it was too warm for red wine today. The little orphans followed the beautiful creature like a trail of ants. He watched them as they giggled and tried to match her graceful style. Poor little urchins. They didn't stand a chance whilst being overshadowed by her glorious image. One of the children turned to Bobby obscuring his view of Estela, "Uncle Bobby," he allowed them that. He thought it would be nice for them after ridding them of that creepy priest. He supposed he was the nearest thing they had to a father now. "can we have some more bleach?" What? "I beg your pardon little man?" Suddenly the small child's eyes appeared to be rotting inside the sockets. Worms pushed through from the skull and dropped out in front of Bobby. "Get away with you! Retched child!" Bobby used the beer bottle to try and put some distance between him and the boy, but the child opened his mouth in response and pushed in closer, "Please Uncle Bobby, can we all have more bleach?" The worms began to force their way out of the decomposing juvenile skull, worse still the other children were filing in behind the first. He couldn't even see Estela now. Bobby tried to stand but the sand wouldn't allow it, his legs struggling for purchase. "Get back I tell you! Damn children! You ungrateful little beasts! Get back I say, let me see your mother." The children instantly divided themselves into two groups, one to the left and one to the right allowing Bobby to watch the angelic form of his woman once more. She carried on dancing with her back to him, apparently unaware of the decomposing children. "Estela! Estela darling. Please sort your children out. That's a good girl, remember we talked about this. Please take them away! I implore you!" The girl carried on swaying her hips this way and that. "Estela!" The figure stopped dancing immediately and slowly started turning around. "Who is Estela?" said the rotten face. "Who? Who are you? Where's my Estela? You… you monster!" The clear sky had turned red, the sea had started to boil and the once golden sand became soot black cutting into his bare skin like a million shards of glass. "Don't you want me Bobby? I thought you loved me?" As the walking corpse came closer to him, Bobby could make out her former features. "No! No, it can't be you!" She glided closer still, "Who is Estela, Bobby?"

He woke up unable to scream. The bedsheets were soaking wet with sweat and fuck knows what else. Bobby even checked to see if he'd shit himself, he was surprised to find he hadn't. What the fuck was that all about? Bobby controlled his own dreams – nobody got to fuck with his subconscious but him! And what was that thing? Christ, it had stolen his beautiful Estela's face away. Bobby tried to think of his Spanish princess, but he just couldn't recall her face. That, thing just kept coming back to him. Right! Well fuck all that thank you very much! He put it down to the emotion of being back in England, seeing his old haunt and the distress he was probably feeling saying goodbye to Emily. The Viagra hadn't helped either. But if he was honest, he'd be glad when it was all over so he could see his beautiful Estela again. Oh, the stories I will tell her!

Bobby didn't fancy going back to sleep again so he checked the time – a little after five in the morning. He wouldn't have slept for much longer as it was, so showered and packed his few belongings. At this time of morning there wasn't many people about and even better, the service desk was left unmanned. The wealthy were far too trusting – all the car keys collected by the valet hung on a board behind reception. Bobby located his own and swapped them for a key engraved with the Mercedes emblem. He did so hope the owner appreciated German automobile history. He reflected for a moment before deciding to mix up a few more keys. Better to be safe than sorry.

Finding the car hadn't been a problem once he'd located the car park to the rear of the hotel. Some SUV of no real note to Bobby, but it was definitely more innocuous than the cherry red classic. That eased Bobby's nerves somewhat, he hadn't been feeling quite right since he woke up. The dream had really disturbed him – Who was that girl? Bobby changed the number plates over with a car of the same year and wasted no more time getting away. Apart from a stop for petrol, breakfast bars and takeaway coffee, Bobby only wanted to get to Colney and to Emily's grave. He came close to making a scene at the petrol station when he couldn't find the button to open the car's petrol tank, but aside from that his journey was uneventful. He saw the first sign for Colney and started looking out for anything that resembled a church. Bobby did like the idea of dropping in on the Chilcot's. Surprise! But that seemed an unnecessary risk now. This was Chilcot's patch, his area. Bobby could respect that and most important – he wanted to live. Maybe one day he'd come back. Renegade on a deal will you? Ha! I had the last laugh!

All he'd seen for a while was more fields and stone walls but now, he was beginning to see the sporadic building. Bobby drove further through the village seeing the houses become more densely clustered. A road sign indicated the church was up ahead on the left behind an old country pub – The Ivy Tavern. It lived up to its name, the brickwork barely visible through the green creepers. Locals walking the street focused their attention on the unknown car, the stares unsettled Bobby. He was happy to see the church and adjoining graveyard as he pulled the car around the corner and stopped. Bobby grabbed the dishevelled cheap flowers he'd picked up from the garage. He hoped to find something more fitting but the uneasy feeling that threatened him all day deterred a visit to the village florist. He would – she would – have to make do. Pushing open the gate and walking into the cemetery was easy but locating Emily's grave was kin to finding a vegan in a butcher's shop. He decided to start looking for newer gravestones when he passed a fellow mourner. The man of around thirty looked at Bobby with an air of suspicion.

"You alroight?" the thick west country accent oozed. Bobby now noticed the man had a terrible overbite and his eyes had no place being so close together. He imagined the gene pool was very small around these parts.

"Hello sir. I do hope I'm not intruding. I'm new to these parts you see but I'm looking for the body of Emil… Sorry. I'm looking for the grave of Hannah…" He'd never been able to remember her full 'true' name. He went with all he had, "Erm… Chilcot maybe?"

"I know who you mean. Fifth row back, eight along. Triffic girl she was. Thought maybe once we mighta had somefunt."

Bobby hid his anger well – this was no place for trouble. Let the man mourn in peace.

"I find that completely implausible but well done. Thank you, kind sir. I bid you a good day," Bobby turned on his heel and followed the man's directions to the grave.

He found himself staring at a family plot of tombstones, the ages of which varied judging by their different stages of erosion. Bobby had no interest in the Chilcot family tree so skipped to the newest looking stone presuming it to be Emily's. He read the inscription with much interest.

Charles Chilcot

72 Years old

Beloved Husband to Alice Chilcot

Uncle to Hannah Parkhurst

So, the old fucker was dead! Ha! Bobby was off the hook then, surely? It did irk him somewhat that he wouldn't be able to surprise the backstabbing prick or have his revenge. But it was still good news, the strange mood that followed him from the hotel bed vanished. He was feeling almost jovial before remembering the real purpose of his visit.

Bobby looked at the other engravings finding Emily – Hannah – and bowed his head. He hoped he was doing it right.

"Hello Emily. It's me, Bobby. I know that's not your real name, but it was the name you gave me and that's got to count for something. I'm sorry I haven't come before now. It's complicated but you need to know that I've held you in my heart ever since that rat took you away from me. Oh, what we could have been together. I would have made you my wife. You'd have liked that. But it wasn't to be, my darling Emily. No. And now I must tell you, I have moved on. I am sorry but I know you would be happy for me. Her name is Estela, you would have liked her. Bit young perhaps, but she's got time. We both have," Bobby couldn't think of much else to say. He'd expected a little bit more, but he had to admit that the little chat had done him wonders. He couldn't even remember what the girl looked like. Instead he pictured Estela. Fuck! There she was again! The rotten girl had taken the place of Estela's and laughed at him with a sickeningly gaping mouth, He couldn't place the features of the girl, but he knew that face! Bobby opened his eyes, shaking his head to rid himself of the image. He was done here. Dropping the cheap flowers on her grave, he turned to leave when he realised that an older woman was staring at him in astonishment.

"Bobby Cavendish. You're meant to be dead!" Alice Chilcot trembled with rage.

"Not looking too bad for a corpse, am I?" he grinned. Well, this had turned out quite nicely indeed. What a nice little catch up. Without the famous Chilcot, Bobby could have some fun with this one. How long did he have before his flight departed?

"Phipps! He fucking promised! He told Charley it was done." He actually felt quite sorry for the poor thing watching her unravel in front of him.

"Well you see Madame, what you've just discovered is that these police types are nothing but a bunch of deceitful pigs, especially in these parochial places. Let's be honest now, your Charlie was just as bad as Phipps. At least Phipps put an end to the killing. He deserves that much," he was enjoying the sound of his own voice so didn't notice the mourner from earlier walking up behind him or the crowd who had left the nearby pub.

"How much? How much did you pay him? Phipps wouldn't have done it otherwise. Charlie was like a father to him. How dare he deny my husband his last wish!" Bobby only now become aware that the exchange was beginning to draw the crowd. He didn't see the young man behind him who was clutching a pitchfork.

“”And how dare you come to her grave! This place isn’t for you. You are the reason she’s here. You are the reason he’s here!”

“Now you listen here Madame. I loved that girl very dearly, she loved me!” He was beginning to lose his cool, the early feeling of unease was creeping up his spine again. To his surprise Alice started to laugh at him.

“Love you? Ha! That’s very funny Robert, very funny indeed. You don’t know love. Charlie knew love, you know hate and fear and power. But you have none of that here, these are Charlie’s people. My people. You are not welcome here Robert Cavendish.”

Tears threatened to burst from his eyes. This old crone didn’t know him! How dare she? Bobby just wanted out of here now. Why the hell had he bothered anyway? It was Estela he loved – these buried bones meant nothing to him. Bobby looked over his shoulder at the lad holding the farming tool and the approaching crowd. He didn’t fancy his chances, but then he did have one ace left up his sleeve – or his chest pocket.

“Get back you webbed fingered fuck!” He aimed the handgun at the mourner which made the crowd halt in their tracks. They hadn’t quite got as far as his car yet, so he made his way down the cemetery path toward the gate keeping the gun trained on his nearest attacker. As he shuffled past Alice, he quickly grabbed her redirecting the barrel of the gun at her head.

"They'll stop you Robert. You know they will."

"Shut up! They try anything and I will happily send you to join your corrupt husband in hell." Bobby forced Alice to walk, the pace slow due to her prosthetic leg. The man with the pitchfork followed them at a meter's pace away. Finally, they made it to the gate and then the car. Bobby released his hand from around Alice but kept the gun pointed at her head. He used his free hand to open the car door and dived through, quickly shutting and then locking the doors behind him. The crowd instantly descended upon the vehicle as Bobby struggled to get the keys into the ignition. Hard projectiles, some already somehow alight bombarded the outside of the SUV as he fired the engine into life. He took no notice of the bodies standing in front of the car as he accelerated away, the wheels bounced and crushed over them, tearing skin and bone. He raced out of the hamlet until he was sure that nobody followed him. Fucking hell, Bobby old son! That had been a near miss and nearly bested by a woman too! One thing was for certain – Bobby was going home – for home is where the heart is.

Phipps Slips

Too distracted by his current dilemma, Phipps declined the invitation to play golf. For the foreseeable future, Austin Healey would be his prime focus. Phipps had tried the number Austin left with his office, but the line went straight to answer phone. It was time to call Bragg. Just the thought of talking to the brown-nosed Bragg repulsed him – needs were musts.

"Chief Constable, what do I owe the pleasure?" Bragg answered in his usual slimy manner. Phipps did his best to ignore it.

"Hello Bragg, I trust you are well. I won't keep you long," Phipps rushed through the conversation knowing that if he gave Bragg half a chance then the mundane man would want to tell him about his wife and children, "How are things going with our nosey little detective constable?"

"Thank you, sir, I'm very well thanks. I have also dealt with the Detective Healey situation and if I'm honest Sir I think he's taking it pretty well."

"Yeah? How so? Has he dropped the case?"

"Well yes I believe so Sir. Austin called in earlier, he's even booked himself a holiday. To the Costa Del Sol of all places. Very unlike Healey, he's a bit of a loner if I'm honest Sir. I think it'll do him some good. I always saw him as more of a caravan man myself."

Hmm. It was a big area of Spain and very popular with tourism but, hmm. He also didn't believe that Austin had given up his investigation that easily. He'd only been talking to Mrs McKay in Colney the day before. Surely, he couldn't know about the villa – could he?

"When did he leave Bragg?"

"Not until this afternoon Sir. Can I ask why Sir? Has Austin been poking his nose about again?"

Phipps had to divert the man. He couldn't have Bragg knowing anything about the villa and who lived in it, "What? No! No, of course not Bragg. Actually, I wondered if you could get him to call me once he's back. I think he might be able to help me with an old investigation. Let him know his cooperation would be well noted. Thanks Bragg," Phipps hung up before the man could respond. Hmm, this was very worrying. He needed Austin here, but he couldn't risk him sniffing around Spain. That's if Austin wasn't just on holiday, which was more plausible than him discovering Bobby Cavendish. Wasn't it? If Austin Healey did find Bobby, then Phipps didn't fancy the man's chances. That would take care of one problem but, what would Bobby do if he thought Phipps had turned him in? The problem was taken away from his hands by the incoming phone call – Alice.

"Alice. How can I help?"

"Alan, we need you to come now. There's been some… developments."

"Alice it's not good timing, I need just a little bit more time to locate our friend."

"Forget him Alan. Do you want the job or not?"

Phipps very much wanted the job, "Yes! More than anything Alice. All I do is to serve you and the community." He'd have to take a gamble on this Austin.

"Then you better come now… We're all waiting for you."

A Room with a View

He watched the young man sitting in the chair, positioned just so. It still wasn't right – It never was. Sometimes Quinlan wondered if he'd ever be able to create the same image again such was his need for his perfect artistic impression – there were no paintbrushes here. He knew he didn't have much longer with this one. The lad had already complained about the cold chair on his naked backside and the goosepimples threatened to destroy the already tainted view. Reluctantly then he gave in, it was time to pay the boy – let him go. It just wasn't to be. He'd have to start the search again. A fresh canvas.

"Okay, that's enough now. Get dressed. Your money is on the table."

The young naked man hopped up off the chair, there was something in the movement but only a flash. No. Quinlan was right to cut this one loose.

"You sure? You've got another ten minutes. I could give you a quick blowie if you like. I mean you pay by the hour either way," the boy paused clutching his clothes waiting for an answer.

Finally, no longer looking in the boy's direction, Quinlan replied, "No. That won't be necessary. You may take your leave."

The lad started to dress, shrugging his shoulders before adding, “Do you want to take my number for next time?”

“No… There won’t be a next time.” The lad finished putting on his clothes and picked the money up but whispered, “Suit yourself,” shutting the door behind him.

Quinlan went to the hotel’s bedside table and picked up his phone, setting it back on full volume. A message on the screen told him he’d missed something urgent. He dialled the number back without hesitation.

“Control,” said the voice on the other side of the line.

“It’s DCI Quinlan. You have something for me?”

“Christ Guv. We’ve been trying to get hold of you for nearly an hour. A body has been found at the Gatwick Travel hotel. I’ll send over the correct address. Sounds like one for your lot. You’d better get over there ASAP.”

“Cheers,” DCI Quinlan replied before ending the call.

Well, I’d better get to it then.

It Was Real

Despite his recent naughty streak, Austin decided it would still be best to put in a request for his leave. It wouldn't hurt to show Bragg some respect and having it on record where he was going looked less suspicious – he hoped – plus it was a good call if anything bad happened. Jules had booked the flight and hotel for him in her name. In truth he didn't plan on staying at the hotel if possible as it was merely a diversion just in case anybody was watching his movements. It had been tempting to take the angel whom he'd woken up next to along. They could make use of the hotel room, not leaving for days, just like Lennon and Yoko. Common sense had won out in the end and Austin swung by his flat to collect a few belongings before departing to the airport alone. It was quite an experience for him as he'd only ever been so far as on a ferry to the Isle of Wight before now, boarding an aeroplane, for the first time, came in with nerves and excitement – much like his previous evening!

Austin followed the on-board safety instructions to the letter, hanging on the flight attendant's every word. He took particular note of the sick-bag location. After a tense ear popping take-off where Austin had dug his nails in to the arms of the chair, eyes clamped shut and scaring the living shit out of the young child next to him – he found himself calm, save for the odd bit of turbulence. He yawned as the plane gently shook him to sleep, they had gone at it again last night and Austin was pleasantly knackered.

XXX

Austin awoke, a strand of saliva hanging between his chin to his shirt snapped as he lifted his head. The plane was shaking – this can't be right! – to add to the panic there was a persistent high-pitched noise, a building pressure in his ear drums. Austin was certain that his head was about to explode. He looked about the plane carriage, nobody seemed to be taking any notice as they calmly packed up their laptops, books or tablets. He turned to the passenger next to him, a young girl who stared at him in wonder.

"Is it okay? Is this normal? Are we going to die?" he spluttered at the inquisitive face.

"It's okay Mr, the pilot is just landing the plane."

"Oh, good. But about this pain in my ears?!"

The girl stuck her hand into her backpack and pulled out a wrapped boil sweet, "Here, suck this. They help."

Austin took the sweet unravelling it frantically and sticking it in his mouth. "Thank you," he managed between sucks. Both ears popped, and with each swallow the pressure eased – what is this sweet elixir?

With the reassurance from a child who probably hadn't even seen her tenth birthday, Austin survived his first plane flight. The return flight will be better he told himself. He'd packed light so didn't have to work out the luggage pick-up and headed straight for the vehicle hire. Jules had seen to that too, booking him a tidy little Jeep – white. A bit edgy for his usual taste but Jules insisted, she promised he would suit the 4x4 with the roof down. That's one of the many things that made him… love? her. Jules saw him differently to other people and most importantly how he saw himself. They'd only known each other a few days but already he was growing the confidence to break out of his shell. He also loved the way she regularly texted her words of encouragement. Austin couldn't wait to get back to see her – he loved Jules.

Left-hand drive had taken some getting used to, but Austin arrived at his hotel, just for the token check-in and to drop off his spare clothes, again, covering his tracks. Suddenly, two naked males in their early twenties ran through the foyer. The one with a rubber ring around his waist chanted "Leeds! Leeds! Leeds!" in the relevant northern-English accent. Austin was now even more certain he would not be staying any longer than necessary. He made a quick visit to his room before heading straight back out to the Jeep. It was early evening and the sun was still out; the villa less than an hour's drive. If he got what he came for he might even be able to catch a late flight back to Jules. Austin connected the Jeep's stereo to his phone and selected 'The Mutts' album, Life in Dirt – it was the perfect driving music. Blasting out of the open top vehicle, life then took him away from the town and all its usual tourist attractions. Before he knew it, Austin was off the beaten track and into the numerous chains of mountains, jutting from the landscape like protruding ribs. It hadn't all been chance – Austin was a great fan of satellite navigation systems, his one condition when Jules booked the vehicle. He followed the sweeping roads, completely desolate except for that one out of control moped. It had come around a blind corner very nearly making Austin shit himself – he became highly aware of the steep drop and lack of safety barriers after that. The road began to decrease its incline and Austin found the landscape opening into fields illuminated in golden orange light, the sun handing over to dusk. He followed the sat nav's directions driving through a small settlement. Austin stared in wonder at the time capsule of a town. Apart from a tractor, he saw no cars or vehicles whatsoever. The people were dressed like the pictures he'd seen in books from bygone days. Chickens ran feral over the dirt track road that separated the settlements. A small group of children ran alongside the car as their elders looked up with little interest. You have reached your destination – The satellite system had nothing else to offer Austin – so he slowed the car, and let the children catch up.

"Hello… erm, let me see… Hola, ¿puedes ayudarme?" He hoped his Spanish was rehearsed enough and that the children could help him.

"Hola señor. ¿Qué tienes? Tú pagas, nosotros ayudamos."

Austin's Spanish was far from fluent, but it didn't matter when the apparent alpha of the children rubbed his fingers together. A universal signal for money – fair enough – he wouldn't be needing the euro's anyway.

Handing over a twenty, Austin started to parley, "I… am… looking… for... a... big... house… like… a… villa… Englishman… live… there… like… me… Englishman… where… house?" The children looked about one another giggling and exchanging words. Austin supposed it didn't matter how slowly he said the words. The leader of the group came back to him once again rubbing his fingers. This time Austin held out the note but pulled it away as the boy reached out. He'd always wanted to do that having been on the receiving end of such torment his entire life. Austin tried a new tactic – the villa was surely up ahead. The road only ran one way, so he used his other hand to point and waved the note with the other.

"Villa, house, er, er… Casa! English man erm… allí vive." Austin's GCSE skills seemed to have got him a reaction. The children talked excitedly amongst themselves. Once again, the fearless negotiator stepped up.

"¿Un loco? Sí, loco inglés. Veinte euros y te llevamos a mitad de camino."

Austin knew loco was crazy, ingles was English and veinte was twenty – euros being obvious. The children certainly seemed to understand him and began ushering him forward, so he handed the head boy the money and followed on. A couple of the adults in the village shouted and shook their disapproval at the children but they ran on ahead regardless. Austin couldn't help but feel a little bit 'Pied Piper' about the whole thing, but never had he been so close to the truth. Be it Paul Hargreaves or someone else, whoever lived up there had clearly gone to a lot of effort to not be found. He followed the children out of the village and into woodland. The road started to climb again this time through a canopy of trees. They finally came to an opening as the landscape gave way to fields. In the distance Austin could make out the faint outline of a white walled settlement on the backdrop of more trees. The children had stopped running now and showed an air of unease about them. Austin stopped the car as their leader approached. The boy indicated to the ground and shook his head, pointing at himself and the others. Austin understood bits of what accompanied the hand gestures. No. We stop. The boy looked towards the building in the distance, “Loco, inglés,” and left him alone, the other children following their commander. They were clearly unsettled by the villa or the ‘loco’ English man who lived there. Austin wondered if he had anything to worry about himself. But then, if he’d been living here for five years he’d go mad too.

Austin took in the view of the well-presented villa driving ever closer. He noticed the gates were open and deliberated whether he should pull in or not, opting to park just outside instead. The gaping entrance seemed to put him on edge as it conflicted with the security conscious high exterior walls. The lack of lighting in the interior of the building wasn’t promising. The sun had all but set leaving little natural light in the sky before the moon started its circle. Austin took a torch with him but sensed he wouldn’t get anywhere tonight if the building was empty. Leaving the car lights on for extra illumination he headed through the entrance. The front of the property was vacant of any vehicles – another bad sign. Austin walked towards the villa itself, wary of the crunch his feet made on the stones. The silence had him on edge.

Beep beep – Beeb beeb

He jumped in fright to the audible alert shattering the silence unable to place where the sound had come from. After he'd calmed himself, Austin remembered his phone was still connected to the open top Jeep's speakers. Clearly it had just been a text – hopefully from Jules… Austin walked to the villa door, noting that none of the windows were drawn shut, evident proof it was very unlikely anybody was home, but all the same, Austin had come too far. His fist knocked on the door, a solid bang that he followed up. The door swung inwards. Austin stepped inside. The first thing he noticed was the man asleep in a deck chair against the opposite wall. The next thing he took in was the old bed sheets hung from floor to ceiling. The logical assumption was that the man had fallen asleep whilst decorating. Except for the ceiling – Why would they cover the ceiling?

Bang!

Austin reacted to the sound before the stinging in his back. If my back hurts, then why is my chest bleeding? He was too good a policeman not to see that he'd been shot and gave in to his buckling knees – he didn't really have a choice. As Austin dropped forward on to his face and the white sheet, the life force draining from his body he realised one thing. It was all that mattered – what he and Jules had – It had been real.

So Long and Thanks for All the Black Pudding

The last time Bobby Cavendish left the 'Homeland' it had been a bitter pill to swallow. He knew at the time staying wasn't an option. Chilcot and Phipps could've buried him, instead of Paul Hargreaves – or as well. Over the last five years Bobby had wondered whether it would have been worth his death, just so that he could avenge her himself. There wouldn't have been enough time in the world for what he had planned for Hargreaves. But today had changed everything. No longer did he have feelings for the rotting corpse buried in that strange little village. No longer would he swap his freedom for her memory – now there was another.

Bobby had floored it out of the village as quickly as the SUV allowed him through the vein of tight country roads. Finally, he'd put some good miles between himself and the twisted village. Bobby Cavendish feared no man – that was until today. He'd certainly feared the man with the pitchfork, the vigilant crowd and most of all that woman! The thought crossed his mind that perhaps he should let Phipps know about the visit; it passed quickly. Well, he was shot of them now – mostly.

Somewhere between Colney and Gatwick, Bobby stopped to fill the car up. A fellow motorist at the adjoining pump alerted him to the mess,

"Bloody pheasants hey mate?" said the stranger pointing at the front of the car, "Looks like it's left a nasty dent too!" Bobby looked and spotted parts of the more unfortunate villagers hanging from the front grill. "Pheasant! Yes! Big bastard too." Phew. He didn't scrimp when it came to pay for his petrol and ordered the full-works-carwash. Thankfully it was machine operated.

Before ditching the stolen vehicle in the airport carpark, Bobby drove past the nearby travel hotel. The same place he'd last seen JJ and where Mr Big's bloated body lay. Bobby guessed it must be giving off quite the smell by now as he watched the circus of emergency vehicles buzzing around. He wouldn't have much to worry about – I'm nearly home Estela, they can't stop me now! He prayed for an uneventful journey – God forbid if I see that mincer again! Bobby couldn't risk anymore public outbursts. He would be glad to see the back of England – except for the black pudding!

Welcome to the Party `Al

Aside from the uncertainty regarding the nosey little officer, Phipps

was feeling very happy with himself indeed. There'd been a moment after talking to Alice that the job was slipping through his fingers until the welcomed invitation had come his way. Chilcot's widow followed up the last call with a message telling him a room was reserved in his name at the local inn – all expenses paid too! Alice made it very clear that he was to check in and immediately come to the village pub. She was very insistent, claiming that the whole community were eager to meet their new protector. Haha! They will be lining up to buy me drinks! Phipps had met a handful of the locals before on his past visits to the Chilcot's. What was the landlords name again? …Harry! That was it. Phipps imagined they would become good friends following in his former mentor's footsteps. Chilcot had told Phipps that he did most of his work from the Ivy Tavern and he couldn't think of a better office for a retired man of his soon to be crowned status. He knew things could be a bit grisly down there at times but Chilcot assured him those offered as scarecrows were worthy of the punishment. Not that he'd witnessed the celebration himself, despite his involvement in Paul Hargreaves' death. Who was he to question the tradition? An age-old practice that predated even the Roman invasion. At the end of the day, all Phipps cared about was the enormous house he'd been able to snap up for a bargain (after Cavendish's 'contribution) and the cushy job role that promised respect, power and of course – money!

Phipps drove into the village and found the Sun-Yetson Inn easily along the high road. The lady at reception – not a bad old catch – greeted him like he was a celebrity. Phipps was a single man having split-up from his first and only wife some twenty-five years before. He just hadn't been able to put her before his career. But now, well the villagers were his work. He'd make it his business to become more acquainted with this Maggie once the formalities of his induction were out of the way. Phipps had to admit he wasn't the greatest fan of the little bed and breakfast; it was a bit dated for his liking and the stuffed fox on display seemed to be giving off a god-awful stink. Thankfully the contracts were due to be signed and exchanged any day now on his new house so he wouldn't have to put up with it for long.

"Now, Alan. Can I call you that my dear? I don't mean to be so informal, but I feel like I know you already! We're all very excited about our new addition to Colney." The flirting from this Maggie was unmistakable to Phipps.

"Of course, my dear Maggie…" they shared a mischievous giggle – Phipps snorting slightly, "I'm very much looking forward to spending the rest of my days here in your beautiful village. I do hope we can move past 'formalities' as soon as possible."

"Now I'm sure Alice has told you that the whole community are eagerly awaiting their new Chief of Police, but I do request one thing of you Alan. I hope you don't mind me being so forward."

"Yes, I understand my presence is eagerly awaited but for you darling Maggie, I would be only too happy to oblige such a welcoming member of my future flock," Phipps dripped with smarminess.

"Oh good!"

"Now, what can I do for you?"

"It would mean so much to me if we could quickly toast your arrival. Just before everyone else, I'm needed here tonight you see. Poor old Maggie won't get to buy you a drink so maybe we could share a quick sherry?"

"Of course, my dear!" Phipps roared in delight. He was very much enjoying the pedestal to which he found himself upon.

Maggie disappeared through one of the reception's doors leaving Phipps. He was feeling very pleased with himself. That bloody fox stinks though! Maggie returned as Phipps wafted his hand about, if she was offended, she didn't show it. Instead the inn keeper passed him a glass of amber liquid, "To Chief Constable Alan Phipps, I thank you for your upcoming service to Colney. Cheers!" Maggie knocked back her own drink. Phipps assumed they would be savoring their time together, but he followed Maggie's lead draining the glass in one.

"Cheers." Phipps enjoyed the sherry burn its way down to his gut but disliked the bitter taste it left. Maggie took his empty glass and flashed her smile at him, "Would you like me to take your luggage Alan? You can check in later if you like, I'll still be here. Best not keep everyone waiting."

"Thank you, Maggie. That would be very kind. Are you sure you don't mind?"

"Not at all. Now, you get yourself off to the pub."

Phipps drank in the fresh air as he left the inn, ridding his nostrils of the fox's stench. Making his way back to the street, he saw a scarecrow in Maggie's front garden. A very good effort by all accounts he thought admiring it. Chilcot had told him about the festival before, Phipps had thought it earlier in the year. There was a lot he would need to brush up on regarding Colney's traditions if he was going to win the people over. He'd make sure to ask Alice privately about it. Phipps' walk took him down the main high street past other residential dwellings. They all had scarecrows up for the festival – they really do go the extra mile – never did the craftsmanship fail to deliver.

Phipps found himself quickly approaching the Ivy Tavern, the drink he'd enjoyed with Maggie was creeping up on him. At least it would help him with the nerves he was beginning to feel. A large group of people stood outside the pub clearly looking his way, Phipps approached them receiving nods of greeting and returning them with a smile. The group parted to allow him access to the pub and one man stood forward to open the door for him. "Welcome to Colney, Chief Constable."

"Well, thank you kind sir," he replied entering an almost empty room save the bartender and one lady sitting on a table.

"Alice, how wonderful to see you. Quite the welcoming party you have out there," he regretted the last part. Did I sound too cocky?

"Take a seat Alan. We've got a lot to go through tonight," Alice's stony look gave nothing away, but she'd been like that since Charlie passed. Phipps did as he was bid and took the chair.

"Harry," Alice turned to the bar, "Would you mind bringing us a couple of drinks please? Alan will try the Dead-Sheep," turning back to Phipps, "It was Charlie's favorite."

"Wonderful, what was good for Charlie, is good for me."

The barkeeper Harry brought over the two drinks. Phipps noticed the man avoided eye contact with him but nodded politely to Alice.

“Thank you, Harry,” tried Phipps but received no response. He sipped at the beer which was rather delightful except the bitter after taste. Must be a regional thing – he’d get used to it.

“Drink up Alan. We’ve got a celebration later. I hope you don’t mind me calling you to come so soon?”

“Of course not.”

“We just had to have you here with us for this occasion. We couldn’t do it without you… Harry can you bring the chief here another drink please?”

Phipps nearly coughed on the beer he was already glugging – he’d only just started this one!

“Relax Alan. We just want you to feel welcome and it is very nice beer isn’t it?” Harry turned up again. He might as well be serving a corpse! But then he just stood still not leaving Phipps’ side. He looked at Alice questioningly.

“Harry’s waiting for your empty glass Alan,” Alice replied calmly.

Can't they see I've got half a pint left?! Not wanting to offend, he quickly downed the pint and handed over the glass. His head swooned slightly – the beer was very good.

"Excuse Harry, Alan. He's not himself tonight, not after the death of his nephew earlier today," Alice hung her head, a mask of sadness on her face.

"I'm verry sorwy to hear that," Phipps shocked himself with the slur of speech.

"Don't you worry yourself about that Alan. Just enjoy your beer."

Phipps forced a few gulps down as Alice stared at his glass.

"Bring our chief another please Harry."

Phipps didn't argue – he didn't have it in him. When Harry came back, Phipps was prepared and downed the remaining drink in one before accepting the next. Alice was talking about something to do with the scarecrows in the village, but he wasn't listening. Numbness spread throughout his body.

"Drink up Phipps!" laughed Alice.

Phipps did as he was bid putting the glass back down clumsily on the table, a string of saliva hanging from his mouth. He could barely keep himself on the chair. Beer. Fucking. Strong.

“That’s the spirit Phipps! Now, let me begin…”

No Turning Back

The tasks Alvaro had set Estela served to keep her mind busy, but once the last sheet had been hung and every light bulb removed from its bayonet – reality kicked in. Her heart was broken by Diego's untimely death and her sanity hung by a thread more precarious than that which held the sword of Damocles. The hurt and abandonment dragged up, emotions not felt since the death of her father. She always believed that past experiences had hardened her soul and that nothing could be worse. Estela now discovered she'd been wrong all along, if anything she felt more fragile than before. So easily had the façade come crashing down revealing foundations in her mind beyond repair. The teachings of God had educated Estela to believe forgiveness was possible, that she was beyond hate and resentment – until now. The only thing that could begin to repair her soul was revenge. Painful, bloody, drawn-out revenge. Alvaro had made it perfectly clear that she could not be witness to the act itself – it had been non-negotiable – Estela had understood at the time. At least she'd certainly pretended to. Now as her mind had more time to overthink, she wasn't so sure.

Alvaro sent Estela back to the orphanage after the preparations were complete with a clear message to stay away and look after the younger children. It didn't take long before it became apparent that it was the children looking after her. Aside from her own incapacitation, Mikel had everything running smoothly and Estela saw her own despondent feelings impacting the atmosphere – she couldn't even talk to any of them about it yet. Padre had insisted – but staying away from the villa was impossible.

XXX

Estela waited until evening, passing the time between inconsolable grief and waves of anger. Sometimes even aimed at Diego's grave for defending her in the first place to the loco man. It is me who should end this vile man not Padre or anybody else. None of it seemed fair, why should Padre make that decision for her?

Making her way to the villa as the sun slowly started to end its shift, Estela paid mind to be careful. She wouldn't want to risk alerting Alvaro to her presence or the loco man for that matter. They had no idea what time the Brit was returning but assumed he would. Estela wondered if the man had come back already – what if Alvaro's in trouble? Her pace quickened and soon the villa was in sight, seemingly silent and deserted. Estela checked the entire perimeter of the outer walls, completing the circuit as Alvaro had showed her that morning. There were no vehicles at the front of the property and the gates were still wide open, so Estela ventured towards the villa itself. She was careful but boldened by grief and prepared herself for what lay beyond the door.

Estela pushed the door open and stepped into the house, the white sheets still covering floor to ceiling. To soak up the blood and hide DNA he'd told her, although ordinarily Alvaro would have used plastic. Looking around she noticed there was nothing different from when she'd been there earlier – except the wooden chair Alvaro had placed along one wall. On first inspection, Estela thought her padre was dead by the way his body slumped in the chair. She didn't need to walk much closer before she saw the slow rise and fall of his chest coupled with the unmistakable – albeit quiet – snore. Estela nearly shook him awake, so enraged was she by the scene. The only thing that had stopped her was what lay on his lap – the gun. There was no hesitation, she wanted this. With only a slight hint of guilt, Estela left Alvaro to his slumber and headed back out of the villa and into the courtyard. There was a small brick built shed near the main entrance of the building and that was where Estela would wait. Unlike her padre – Estela didn't care if she got caught.

Lord of the Flies

…please Uncle Bobby! Please bury us!" The children had dug themselves a hole in the sand. "That's not deep enough children." They carried on using their little hands to dig but the sand was too fine, the grave just fell in on itself no matter how hard they tried. Bobby found the whole scene hilarious. "Can you bury us now Uncle Bobby?" He laughed again, "No, you need to dig deeper still." One of the boys got up, "I know! We can use something else." A few of the children followed the boy as Bobby looked over to the glorious silhouette of his darling Estela dancing again by the gentle shallows of the sea. The boy returned with his accomplices, bearing rocks as big as they could carry. "You!" said the boy pointing at one of the smaller children, "Lay down in that hole." The smaller child abided instantly as the other children got up away from the grave. "We can bury him with rocks Uncle Bobby! Look…" The boy smashed the rock down into his younger companion's' body the others following suit. "What?! What are you doing? Stop that now you beastly fuckers!" Bobby couldn't stomach the image. One by one the children threw down the rocks, destroying the younger child beyond recognition. The poor recipient lay there complacent from the get-go. "Estela! Come here quick now! See what your children are doing!" She walked up the beach towards them swaying majestically. "Yes, Bobby darling?" He looked back at the grave. The mound of rocks had completely engulfed the poor innocent child underneath. "They just buried that boy! He was a child for fucks sake!" Estela came closer now, her hair wet and hanging across her face, "Bobby, they're burying him for you." Estela stood over Bobby and flicked back her hair unmasking the decomposing face of Emily, "You killed him Bobby. You killed all of us."

Bobby woke up with a start remembering he was thirty-eight thousand feet in the sky. Thankfully he'd been seated in the window seat beside an old couple who were both snoring heavily – he tended to be at his most unpredictable when waking suddenly. That dream though! Was that… Emily? He had to see Estela again. That's all it was, those weird inbreeding cultists had just put the shits up him – that was all. Those horrible kids are freaking me the fuck out. He'd nip any of that shit in the bud when he met these orphans. Bobby had enjoyed enough of his subconscious for now and kept himself awake for the remainder of the journey. Too distracted by the weird feeling left by the dream, Bobby never noticed the blatant signs of disrespect shown by numerous people on his journey to the car park. His mood was cheered slightly by the Spanish heat once he'd departed the airport. The sun had all but disappeared from the sky but still it was warmer than the days back in England. He knew it would be dark before he made it back to the villa so reasoned that a good night's sleep was in order. Tomorrow was a big day, but first thing he would go and see Estela. She must be his. Bobby found his car, a crappy little thing. He despised the white 4X4, but hard times had meant selling his previously lavish all-terrain vehicle. The shitty one he now owned was the cheapest thing that could deal with the unforgiving journey to and from the secluded villa.

XXX

Bobby was long overdue rest by the time he approached the village – the last stop – before his home. He'd been heavily relying on the car's headlights for the last couple of miles but there was no missing the little 'shanty town' as he liked to call it. The glow from the little abodes let him know he was on the last stretch – or was he? He slowed the vehicle as a group of filthy threadbare children waved their hands at him. A dark feeling lurked in Bobby's stomach. One of the children ran alongside the driver's door.

Lay down in that hole

"What do you want, you little cunts?"

The boy ran up closer to Bobby and began to speak in Spanish which was pointless – he hadn't had a chance to look at that handbook yet.

We can bury him with rocks Uncle Bobby!

The children – all of them, unsettled Bobby. He ignored the boy rubbing his fingers together and stepped on the accelerator, quickly getting out of the settlement and leaving the feral children behind him. He had a mind to go back and shoot the little fuckers, but he just wasn't at the races today – the dream had really stuck with him. Bobby remembered a book he'd loved as a child. A rare piece of happiness from his earlier years. A group of boys left to their own devices on a deserted island – Bobby had seen himself as the ringleader – not that fucking poofter who defended the fat kid – No. He was the one who became the chief, the leader… the hunter. Those children back there had threatened all of that for the second time in Bobby Cavendish's day. Was he their beastie? Were they the hunters? He never answered himself because as he drove into the open land leading to his villa, Bobby saw car lights. He turned his off and crept up to the villa on foot once he let the car coast as far as it could. Bobby noticed with amusement, the car was a similar model to his own and the same colour. He took out his handgun having already checked and loaded it and headed cautiously to the gates.

Out of Practice

Alvaro had felt guilty sending Estela home, but it was still his duty to protect her innocence. Of course, he'd seen far worse himself long before he was the girls age. The self-acclaimed holy man had wanted something different for his flock of children. The risk both he and the girl faced if the foreigner came back before he was ready was too strong, he knew it was for the best. The night wasn't far away and he'd finally gave in to his weary body and pulled up a chair. Back in his youthful days, Alvaro could function for two to three days without sleep but was feeling the pull now. He didn't want to accept that his ageing body was letting him down. Think of Diego. The image of the boy's corpse snapped his eyes wide open again – it was getting harder to fight to stay awake. Alvaro reassured himself that his senses were finely tuned, the slightest movement would stop him from dozing. It was probably too early for the loco man to return, maybe he would come back tomorrow? He'd just rest his heavy eyelids – just for a minute.

Bang!

The single gunshot shook him awake in an instant as he realised his error. Instinctively he reached for the gun but couldn't find it on his lap and jumped up from the chair producing his knife. Laying headfirst on the sheeted floor was the bleeding body of a man. Even in the poor light Alvaro knew the man was too short and bald to be the loco man. Sleuthing his way around the room keeping himself hidden from the open doorway, Alvaro made his way to the body in a hope to surprise whoever had fired the shot. It must be him! But who was this other victim? As he neared the entrance, he heard sobbing from outside – Estela!

Alvaro jumped around the partially open door seeing the girl he thought of as his own daughter sobbing on her knees. He saw the gun discarded on the floor beside her – his gun.

"Estela! My dear why? What have you done?"

"Padre… I'm so sorry. I had to do it…" the rest was lost to her crying.

"It's okay. We will deal with it together. Whoever he is." This broke Estela out of her torrent of tears.

"What do you mean Padre? He is the loco man, no?"

"No Estela. No. It isn't him," Alvaro walked over to the girl so that he could comfort her. He was only one step away…

Bang! Bang!

The first shot to his chest didn't kill him but he did drop the knife as the bullet passed through his shoulder. The second entered the center of his forehead taking a chunk of brain and skull with it. Alvaro was dead before his blooming skull hit the floor, careening onto Bobby's 'Welcome Home' doormat.

Innocence Lost

Bobby stayed well hidden from the stranger approaching his villa –

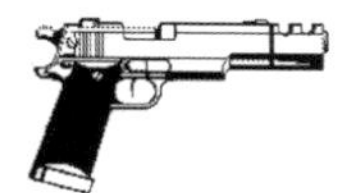

the man looked slightly familiar. *Where have I seen him?* Despite the recognition, Bobby remained in the shadows. The man knocked on the wooden door which swung slowly open. *I didn't leave the bloody door open!* He blamed the children from the village, they'd probably been rifling through his stuff in his absence. Well, he'd soon see to them. Maybe the man was from the village, but Bobby highly doubted it judging by the clothes. Although not to his own high standards they were superior to the rags worn by the locals. The stranger took a step inside the villa and Bobby decided to leave his hiding place stopping abruptly as he saw another figure emerge from behind his coal shed. There was no mistaking her, she was an angel. Curiously Estela clutched a gun with both hands held out in front of her. Before Bobby could process the image, Estela squeezed the trigger at the stranger in Bobby's house. *Good girl! She must have been protecting his villa while he was away. He knew it was meant to be!* Well this was a turn of events indeed! Bobby had expected a bit of wooing would be required – a first date at least – yet here she was practically throwing herself at him with the greatest display of love – murder. Bobby was complete. Estela fell to her knees dropping the gun and beginning to weep. Bobby wanted to run to her and throw his arms around her – it's okay my love. It's okay. You did well. He moved out from the cover and took only a couple of steps before another man arrived in the doorway. At first it had seemed as though the first man must have picked himself up off the ground, but Bobby knew that dead was dead – whoever the fuck he is. No, this man was that son-of-a-bitch priest! Why was he bloody here? The priest called out to Estela moving towards her. Got to show respect to the in-laws I suppose. Bobby would make the effort – the girl was worth it.

… "Quick Uncle Bobby, we need a knife?"

The child's voice boomed inside of his head taking him completely off guard, ducking down and spinning his head around to see if anyone was behind him. Nobody was in close proximity, but he looked on as Estela's father figure approached his girl. Bobby wanted to be there first…

… "Uncle Bobby please! We want a knife. He's got one!"

The voice boomed inside his head taking him off guard once more.

"Who...?" Bobby stopped himself. Speaking the words sobered him. So insane that it was to reply to the voice.

… "That man Uncle Bobby! Quick! He's got a knife! Save mummy!"

Bobby reacted to the voice better this time and looked over towards the priest holding a knife in one hand and approaching the love of his life.

Bang!

Bang!

The first disabled the weapon, the second killed. Bobby was a good shot – he'd had a lot of practice.

Estela stopped crying and looked up – There you go Bobby old son! You've made her happy! He ran over to the girl, she looked at him with beautiful wide brown eyes, the tears made them sparkle like diamonds. Oh, how I wish I had a camera now.

Adoption

The first shot dragged Estela from her self-pity – she'd just killed a man in cold blood – the second shot had torn her last grasp on sanity. The padre's head exploded, the man who had taken both her and her brother after the atrocities they'd endured was gone. He who had shown her unconditional love, understanding and teaching. Had held her hand and comforted her as she divulged to him her most hidden truths. The man who'd brought her together with Diego, had shown Diego the same love. The man who had vowed to avenge Diego for her… had fallen asleep. Untold rage that she'd suppressed boiled to the surface and exploded, but not at the loco man she saw behind her. No. Estela's anger was to Alvaro. He'd failed her but most of all, Diego. She stood up and made her way to his body, if only to vent her emotions. But when Estela saw him lay there, the absolute certainty of death forced her legs back to the ground, knees slamming onto the outer threshold where Alvaro rested. Who would look after them now? Estela leaned down hugging the mangled padre's head awaiting her fate as the footsteps came up behind her. He'd taken everyone else that mattered to her, she would give her life willingly. Kissing what was left of her father's face for the last time, Estela put her hands on the ground to push herself up – to face her maker – her fingers brushed something metallic.

The First Dance

Bobby's heart danced with excitement as he closed upon his one 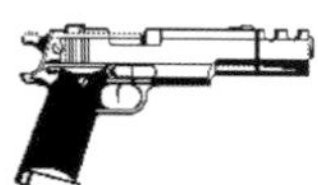 true love. He could understand the mix of emotions the girl was having as she kissed the padre goodbye – that was okay. He would explain the knife later. There was a lot he could offer in the way of experience when it came to shit parents. That was something they both had in common – it really was meant to be. Best yet, she was rising towards him as each step took him closer to what was his. Bobby stretched out his arms, ready for the embrace – she didn't raise her own, but she did stand facing him. Expecting him – this was it. Bobby was nervous, he'd never been this close with Emily. Tonight, he was going one step further to love – this was it. He moved closer – Estela fully erect now in all her splendor. Bobby wrapped his arms around her feeling that she willed it… something was wrong. At first, she felt limp in his arms – there was no warmth – but then – a spark. She wrapped one arm around his waist drawing him in closer – yes! – he watched her other hand that had hung lifelessly moments before reaching up to him, quick with – passion! – he looked into her alluring eyes. They sparkled with lust? – no this isn't right. Was this love? That free hand reached up to his other side and her touch was electric. Estela looked deep into his soul, his retina the window and spoke,

"You killed him Bobby. You killed all of us."

She sounded so fluent – Bobby had never expected such good English. She almost sounds like…

Estela released her grip on him and now the initial sensation of her touch turned to something other than excitement. Now Bobby felt pain and as he clutched his side, he saw blood – lots and lots of blood.

I Get it Now

Phipps' mind had been too distracted by his physical decline. But now it was becoming impossible not to notice the running theme and that's what worried him the most. The widow – Alice – kept talking about things that she should never know. Things that they shouldn't have known. Phipps always thought himself overly cautious when it came to his extra 'funding'. He'd been careful to keep it hidden from Charlie – mostly – he wouldn't approve. The widow was making him question that now.

"Alan, he'd been watching you for years! Even after he left the force. You were his prodigy. Christ, he used to talk about you all the time when you worked together. You were like a son to him, that's the only reason he let it go. I know there is no way we could ever blame you for dear Hannah's death, wouldn't dream of it. However, you enabled him… Bobby-fucking-Cavendish. And even then, Charlie still said, 'let it go', 'he's a good man'. Charlie always saw the best in you. Right up to the end he still believed in you, even on his death bed with the tubes snaking out of him. The respirators keeping him alive just for one more hour that I could be with him. He still asked for you, his dying wish 'Kill Cavendish'… You would have redeemed yourself in his eyes, perhaps even in all of us. You would have become Colney's protector."

Bobby-fucking-Cavendish – how had he fucked this up? Phipps might not be able to control his body, or mouth, or much – but, he did know that he was fucked. Proper fucked. All Cavendish had to do was stay the fuck away! He wondered if that Austin Healey had something to do it. I should have bloody dealt with him. Either way – Phipps was fucked. The poison that flowed through his veins was paralysing him. He knew what this meant, the villagers saw him as the enemy, but why? How could they know about Cavendish? Surely, he wouldn't have risked exposing himself. Phipps had kept Chilcot's death a secret from Bobby but then he hadn't had anything to do with the former Bristol enforcer for many years now. Not since his little visit to the Costa Del Sol some four years ago where they had come to a suitable agreement. Bobby had made a healthy contribution to Phipps' retirement fund in exchange for Phipps' word that he would tell Chilcot, Bobby Cavendish was no more. Phipps had no affection for Bobby, truth be told the man scared the shit out of him. Every minute he'd spent in that villa alone with him had been on a knife's edge. The relief when he got back on the plane was phenomenal. That was when Cavendish had needed Phipps to get the hidden money that would benefit both parties. Their relationship when Phipps allowed Bobby Cavendish to run the criminal underworld under his jurisdiction had been very different. There was no one-on-one encounter for a start, just the odd call from a burner phone to let him know where to find his monthly cut. The drops had become much lighter and less frequent over the last two years of Bobby's reign which is when Phipps knew it was time to send in another mole. He needed someone who wouldn't be afraid to get his own hands dirty. But Hargreaves had got too ahead of himself and killing the girl! If Hargreaves had been honest with him about it from the off, he might have been able to deal with it. Perhaps Chilcot wouldn't have even found out about his niece's employment in Cavendish's empire. Phipps found that his own past had caught up with him – he would be sharing the same fate as his previous sergeant.

But how do they know about Bobby Cavendish? He wouldn't have to wait much longer for an answer as Harry the barkeeper walked over to the pub table. He waited patiently for Alice to stop talking.

"Okay Phipps. You've had enough," Alice turned to Harry, "You can take him now, thanks Harry. It's time." Harry picked up Phipps' limp body from the chair, chucking him over his shoulder with ease. They left the pub and again the crowd outside made way for Chief Constable Phipps. Slumped over the barkeeper's back, Phipps looked at the waiting crowd who returned his gaze with an animalistic hunger. Alice led the way across the street to the graveyard. Yes, I thought this was probably where they did it. Phipps knew with certainty that he was going to die a painful death for what he'd done – or not done. As the procession followed Alice, Harry and the new offering through the cemetery gates, Phipps saw two freshly dug graves. He tried to move his head in the same direction when Alice noticed.

"Not for you Phipps. Only the pure are buried here. Those graves are for two of your victims, one of them was Harry's daughter."

Phipps didn't know what she was on about. He may have been a lot of things but a murderer he was not.

"Not you personally," Alice seemed to read his thoughts, "Bobby Cavendish decided to pay us a visit yesterday. We hoped he would give you some company tonight but unfortunately, he managed to escape. Not without crushing two of our own to death in the process."

So that's how they knew – Fucking Cavendish! Egotistical maniac! Why had he come back?

"He'll be back. We always get our man Phipps."

Helped by another villager, Harry tied Phipps to a wooden stake. Binding his legs to the upright and stretching his arms out horizontally securing them to the cross. He didn't need to be an expert in Colney folklore to know what was coming. Phipps tried to beg but the effort to piece his words together was just too much – his mind followed suit, losing the battle to remain conscious.

A New Hope

DCI Joseph R. Quinlan studied the naked boy. The angle, the lighting – the similarity was strikingly close. Close but not right. Quinlan tried to let his eyes relax on the recreation who abided his request – not without question, however. This young specimen certainly had an annoying ability to query everything. It had taken some time to make the boy settle down and remain silent. He succumbed in the end – they usually did. It puzzled Quinlan why the boy was so curious, suspicious of what was being asked of him. He had no doubt that in the boy's usual line of work that this was a relatively easy job, demanding no physical effort and a far cry from his regular customers – it sickened Quinlan to think of himself as such. It's no good. I won't see him this time, best to let the lad go. Just like he had with the one before and the one before that and so on. How many have there been now? It didn't matter. It would take as long as it took until he found him.

"You can get dressed now. Thank you for your time, money is on the side."

The boy bounced up from the chair, rubbing his naked arse cheek, "Thank god for that! Me bum was going proper numb as well. Is that really all you wanted me to do then luvvy?"

"Yes, thank you," Quinlan averted his eyes out of respect as the boy started to dress.

"Well everyone's got their 'thing' I spose! You ain't the first strange one I've had this week either! Bloody ell, you shoulda seen this other one, mind you, he wasn't exactly a customer. In fact, he paid me to piss off so he could take one of my regulars. When I asked him why, he started getting all protective like. Real strange he was. Definitely didn't seem gay to me but then neither do you. Not that I'm bothered. Probably lost me regular now though, I ain't heard from him all week, not since I gave that fella my room key for the travel hotel…"

Quinlan had been filtering the boys voice out of his mind until the last part – about the hotel.

"Where was this?" It was only a hunch, but Quinlan was a good detective. He might be the best.

"Oh, just that one near the airport on the main road. Nothing special but I still had to go slum it up with a girlfriend for the night."

"What night did this happen lad?"

"Oh, please! Call me JJ. Well, let me see. It would have been two nights ago now. Yeah. The fella who took my place had just returned to

England with me. We were sitting right next to each other on the plane… I'll be honest he was a bit of a bore to start with."

Could this man be of interest to Quinlan? Surely there was too much of a coincidence for this to be ignored – he pushed on.

"JJ Would you be able to tell me either of their names? Who was your client?"

"Sorry, I'm like totally confidential with that sort of thing you know."

DCI Quinlan pulled out his badge showing it to the half-dressed lad.

"You? You're a bloody copper? What is this? You catching me out or something? No wonder why you only watched." The boy started looking about the room, presumably for cameras.

"No. Not at all JJ, you have nothing to worry about. What we did here today was… something… else. I'd appreciate you keep it between us, its… complicated. Listen JJ, have you seen the news?"

"No, I don't watch it, too bloody depressing. Why?"

"There was a body found in that hotel, it's probably unrelated but you would really be helping me out if you could give me a name."

"What about me though? I don't want to get myself wrapped up in all this. Your lot are homophobic as it is, don't want to be the little rent boy that gets murder pinned on him."

"JJ, I promise you. I would really prefer to keep what happened here today between us. I'm sure you can see why this might reflect badly on a police officer. You help me and I'll keep your name out of this."

JJ considered the deal but didn't need long to make up his mind. What choice did he have? "Okay. Well my customer was Mr Big, you probably know him as Mark Barret who owns that football team..."

That's him! That's the victim.

"…and the other bloke I don't know his name, but he was on the same flight as me… hang on!" JJ pulled on his t-shirt and reached into his jeans pocket pulling out a mobile phone, "Yeah! I think I got him in the background of this selfie me and my bestie took." He swiped the screen a few times before handing it to Quinlan, "Here! That's him."

Quinlan took the phone and stared past the image of the grinning JJ and his female companion. There was no mistaking the face who sat behind them. Quinlan knew those blue eyes, the handsome face, the sharp looking suit – he'd recognise Bobby Cavendish anywhere – even if he had died over five years ago.

Retirement Party

Phipps awoke to darkness and quickly remembered where he was –  and why. Some of the feeling was coming back to his body now, but it wasn't enough to try and wrestle himself free of the wooden cross. Looking at his bound arms, he noticed the hay and straw stuffed inside of his clothes, the oversized hat that hung slightly over his face and the strong smell of petrol. He didn't have to rely too heavily on his policing skills to deduce he was a scarecrow. Phipps also knew what the petrol meant – they really were going through with it. His heart started beating rapidly willing his body back to life. A shadow passed at the corner of his vision. He could hear voices, lots of them approaching and sure enough a large group of locals came around the corner and headed into the graveyard. Most of them brandished burning torches led by her, the widow. The front of the crowd had almost reached him, Phipps' eyes struggled to adjust to the light. He tried to see the faces of the other members. There he was! The figure had vanished into the crowd. Alice walked up to him, craning her neck back admiring the presentation.

"You look very good Alan. It was a community effort, we're very happy with the results."

He screamed inside his skull at them to stop, take pity on him. This is fucking crazy! I'm being killed for not killing. Had any of his crimes ever warranted this?

Alice was the first to lay down her torch on to the unlit fire below. Phipps could see that the flames wouldn't take long to reach his feet.

"He wouldn't have wanted this for you Alan, but I do. Not covering your tracks and bringing it to Colney was one thing, but allowing that fucking animal, Bobby Cavendish to live? You promised Charlie and now not only have you failed him you're the reason that bastard was alive to come here. Goodbye Phipps…" Over her shoulder, it was him again – smiling. "You are my first offering! A worthy one I'd say." Alice left as the flames licked up over his feet, melting boots. More feeling was coming back but as it did, untold pain followed. He couldn't even scream. As the next participant in this wicked cult stepped up and dropped their torch and the next one and the one after, Phipps wondered – what separated the villager's actions from the evil Bobby Cavendish? Who was judging the level of wickedness? – Not Phipps. His body had finally given into shock from the roaring fire which climbed his waist. The last thing he saw – him.

Recruit

Alice watched him burn. She knew it wouldn't have been what Charlie wanted, he would have given him another chance. Alice knew though, she knew better. Especially now she watched the man who had failed him – had failed them – burn alive. There was no mercy for anyone who threatened their community. That had been Charlie's problem, he hadn't grown up here. Alice understood what it meant to keep the tradition alive and Colney needed somebody to lead. Due to tradition, a woman would never be able to assume command as Protector but that was just a title. If she could find someone, a police officer of rank who was pliable. Somebody who would be only so happy to obey her command in the name of the late great Charlie Chilcot. Who oversees that nosey little policeman? Phipps had said he'd dealt with it, that would mean he knew Austin's superior. A man who could follow instructions without question. Alice would investigate – Colney needed a new leader.

Lost

Two days later

The texts stopped first. Jules hadn't worried about it too much. Austin would be busy and after the night they'd shared, Jules thought it very possible that Austin needed sleep. That night was the most significant of Jules' adult life – Disneyland had been the other. Never had she been so completely in unison with another person. She didn't want him to leave that morning, at that moment nothing else had mattered. The case was too important, Jules understood what it meant to Austin. But that was two days ago, and she hadn't received any contact from him since. His phone no longer rang only going straight to voicemail. There was always the possibility that he'd used the excursion to move on from her – perhaps he'd found somebody else. However, as much as Jules was her own worst critic it was just so out of character for Austin. On top of that, his weekly blog was due on their mutual birder's web page tomorrow. He'd never failed to deliver. The more Jules thought about it she knew something was very wrong.

Eventually Jules received a message from an unknown number – He's gone. He found someone else. Let him go – when she tried calling the number back nobody answered. Eventually that line had stopped receiving calls too. What had Austin stumbled upon? And who could Jules trust? She had to decide between taking the anonymous message at face value or following her suspicions.

"Give him a few more days dear," Jules' mother suggested. "If he doesn't know what he's missing then forget about him," her father said.

I suppose it was too good to be true... Stupid girl…

Sweatpants

Gary watched Jules' flat for two days. He'd even pulled an all-nighter. Jules hadn't left her flat but better yet, nobody had gone in. He's let you down baby doll. Don't worry, Gary's here for you. To help things along, Gary had purchased a cheap pay-as-you-go phone. He knew the message would hurt at first but given time she would heal. Whatever happened – Gary would be there – waiting.

Epilogue

The waves lapped lazily at the shore. The children appeared happy playing on the beach. He liked watching them when they were in this playful mood. He allowed them to engage with him, they spoke, sometimes, even throwing the odd ball their way. It made him feel complete. There were times when they became intolerable and he would ask her to take them away. That older child would usually take them off and then they could be together. She hadn't been the same after the incident. He tried reassuring her that there was no need to worry about the knife wound, it was only superficial. The love they shared was beyond such trivial matters as murder and language. Estela didn't talk much these days anyway – not that he would have understood her! Ha! Ha! He was so glad they had accepted him into their family – not that they could object. Their 'mother' offered no resistance and the rest of the children followed his orders. The villa had fetched a good price, he promised them a new start. Bobby found them this very nice place by the beach, he did it for all of them. They would be happy here – all of them. Nothing could go wrong.

Acknowledgements and thanks

I would like to thank each and every one who has supported me along this journey. Joe Runnacles, my editor, encourager and beautiful friend. My ever-patient wife Lauren for sharing my joy in the good times and picking me up in the bad. Thank you for your continued support and most of all tolerance. I'm indebted to all of those who took the time to read my early drafts, provide feedback and offer advice. They are; Robin White, Paul Veal, Norman Aspin, Lauren Jenkins, Bam Barrow, Trevor Robinson, Colin Woodgate, Keith Woodgate, Gemma Oakes, Mark Cobb (The plane flight) and so many more.

Hunter and Frankie for being the most understanding children I could ever wish for. Mum, Dad, Amber and Sam for being so supportive.

I reserve special thanks to John Bowie, Matthew McGuirk, Andrew Marsh (Dial Lane Books – Ipswich) and of course Cody Sexton. Thanks to yourself and Red (Alien Buddha Press) for taking a chance on this twisted tale.

James Jenkins

February 2023

About the Author

James Jenkins is a Suffolk based writer of gritty noir fiction. James enjoys spending time with his family, playing guitar and reading books. He has multiple short stories published online or in print at *Bristol Noir, A Thin Slice of Anxiety* and *Punk Noir Magazine* among others. He is the co-creator of the online audio platform Black Shadow Lit.

His debut Novel *Parochial Pigs* was published in early 2022 by Alien Buddha Press and is available from Amazon.

Follow James @

twitter.com/JamesCJenkins4

jamesjenkinswriter.wordpress.com

www.facebook.com/JamesJenkinsAuthor/

Instagram – james_jenkins_writer